NRA CET - Matriculation Pass

General English

Latest Edition
Practice Kit

12 Tests
12 Topic-Wise Test

Topic Wise Chapters with Questions

✓ Thoroughly Revised and Updated
✓ Detailed Analysis of all MCQs

Title : NRA CET - Matriculation Pass General English
Author Name : Mr. Rohit Manglik
Published By : EduGorilla Community Pvt. Ltd.
Publishers Address : 12/651, First Floor Opp. Arvindo Park, Near Jama Masjid, Indira Nagar, Lucknow, Uttar Pradesh-226016, India

Copyright EduGorilla

ISBN : 978-93-55560-78-0
First Edition

Disclaimer EduGorilla

Compiled and created by EduGorilla Community Pvt. Ltd

Printed By EduGorilla Community Pvt. Ltd.

ROHIT MANGLIK
CEO, EduGorilla

Editor's Note

Dear Applicants,

People say *"Success comes to those who work hard."* But I've seen people working hard for their exams day in and day out for marginal success. While others succeed in their examinations by putting in just half the work. So are they God Gifted? No! I believe that it's because they work *smart* and not just *hard*. Similarly, for your exams, you should strategize your preparation so as to increase the likelihood of success. Well with EduGorilla get ready to increase your *chances of selection* in your exam by *16x*.

EduGorilla helps you in not only working *hard* but also working in a *smart and strategic* manner. With EduGorilla's preparation package, you get a chance to make your exam preparation easy, and a fun learning path towards selection. Finding the right path to your preparations can be difficult if you don't know in which direction to head. Don't worry, we have you covered! EduGorilla will be your guide to success in your journey. With our Preparation Package, you can prepare strategically and beat the exam in just one attempt.

EduGorilla's Preparation Package includes-

- **Test Series**
- **Books**

Our preparation package is handcrafted as per the latest changes, expert opinions, and students' discretion. Thus, enabling you to get through each stage of the selection process for your exam.

Our Books are designed by the teachers and experts of the respective exam with a combined 150+ years of experience; to provide you with easy, efficient, and effective learning. Our books are smart, in the sense that not only do they give you the answers to the questions but also provide similar questions for practice.

EduGorilla's competent Test Series gives you real-time experience and confidence through which you can clear your offline or online exam in just one attempt. We currently host 83,000+ mock tests for 1,440+ competitive and academic exams.

Thus, EduGorilla misses no chance to assist you in your preparation and covers all stages of the exam, so that you don't have to look anywhere else.

We provide complete preparation packages for defense, banking, teaching, and other National & State-Level exams. Hence, it doesn't matter which exam you aspire to because you will reach your success.

ALL THE BEST !

Let EduGorilla be your Guide to Success.

Rohit Manglik,
Founder and CEO, EduGorilla

INTRODUCTION

EduGorilla focuses on guiding students to succeed in their examinations. With that in mind, our book, titled "NRA CET - Matriculation Pass : General English", has been drafted through the collective efforts of our distinguished experts with 150+ years of combined experience. This book consists of questions that are created following the latest changes in the syllabus and exam pattern. We compiled the book on the basis of questions that are most likely to appear in the . Through EduGorilla's "NRA CET - Matriculation Pass : General English" your chances of success will increase 16x.

EduGorilla does this through our Complete Preparation Package. This package consists of well-conceptualized and structured content in the form of questions that are tailor-made according to your needs and will help you practice for exams in a smart way by pinpointing all the necessary information. It also provides hints and solutions, along with a smart answer sheet for your self-evaluation. You can assess your shortcomings and work accordingly on areas that may require more of your attention.

EduGorilla promises to help you succeed in your examination and accomplish your dream goals. We believe in our aspirants and see them at the top of the merit list. And the first step towards the top is to start preparing with us. EduGorilla's "NRA CET - Matriculation Pass : General English" includes the following attributes.

➤ Well-Researched Content

➤ Top-Notch Quality

➤ Detailed Answers and Analysis

➤ Smart Answer Sheet

➤ Exam Relevant Questions

Therefore, EduGorilla fortifies your preparation and makes it durable enough to help you stand tall and beat the examination.

TABLE OF CONTENTS

Q.1 Direction: Choose the option that is the active form of the given sentence.

He was hit in the eye by an arrow.

A. An arrow will hit him in the eye.
B. An arrow hit him in the eye.
C. An arrow has hit him in the eye.
D. An arrow was hitting him in the eye.

Q.2 Direction: Choose the option that is the passive form of the given sentence.

You might be promoted this year.

A. They might promote you this year.
B. They will promote you this year.
C. You may promote them this year.
D. They should have promoted you this year.

Q.3 Direction: Choose the option that is the active form of the given sentence.

A new song is being composed by her.

A. She has been composing a new song.
B. She is composing a new song.
C. She has composed a new song.
D. She composed a new song.

Ques (4-7):Direction: Choose the option that is the passive form of the given sentence.

Q.4 The child tore the page of the book.

A. The page of the book was torn by the child.
B. The page of the book tore by the child.
C. The book's page is torn by the child.
D. The page of the book is tearing by the child.

Q.5 The class teacher was taking the children to the zoo.

A. The children will go to the zoo by their class teacher.
B. The children can be taking to the zoo by their class teacher.
C. The children being taken to the zoo by their class teacher.
D. The children were being taken to the zoo by their class teacher.

Q.6 I burnt my hand yesterday while cooking.

A. My hand was burning yesterday while cooking.
B. My hand could be burnt yesterday while cooking.
C. My hand was burnt yesterday while cooking.
D. My hand will be burnt yesterday while cooking.

Q.7 The Municipal Corporation changed the manhole covers before the rainy season.

A. The manhole covers is being changed before the rainy season.
B. The manhole covers are change before the rainy season.
C. The manhole covers were changed before the rainy season.
D. The manhole covers can be changed before the rainy season.

Q.8 Direction: Choose the option that is the active form of the given sentence.

By whom was this poem written?

A. Who wrote this poem?
B. Who is wrote this poem?
C. Who write this poem?
D. This poem is wrote by whom?

Ques (9-11):Direction: Choose the option that is the passive form of the given sentence.

Q.9 The tennis ball hit Dhiraj on the head.

A. Dhiraj had been hit on the head by the tennis ball.
B. Dhiraj was hit on the head by the tennis ball.
C. The tennis ball was being hit by Dhiraj.
D. Dhiraj was being hit on the head by the tennis ball.

Q.10 The fisherman caught a large fish.

A. A large fish should be caught by the fisherman.
B. A large fish was catching the fisherman.
C. A large fish was caught by the fisherman.
D. A large fish had been catched by the fisherman.

Q.11 They need 104 more runs to win the match.

A. 104 more runs are needed for them to win the match.
B. 104 more runs will need for them to win the match.
C. They are needed 104 more runs to win the match.
D. 104 more runs can be needed by them to win the match.

Ques (12-13):Direction: Choose the option that is the active form of the given sentence.

Q.12 Has your message been despatched?

A. Has your message despatched?
B. Have you despatched your message?
C. Had you despatch your message?
D. Is your message despatching?

Q.13 I am sometimes puzzled by her actions.

A. Her actions are sometimes puzzled by me.
B. Her actions sometimes puzzle me.
C. She can sometimes puzzle me.
D. Her actions were sometimes puzzling me.

Q.14 Direction: Choose the option that is the passive form of the given sentence.

Mrs. Vaijanthi teaches us literature.

A. We have been taught literature by Mrs. Vaijanthi.
B. Literature was being taught by Mrs. Vaijanthi to us.
C. Literature is taught to us by Mrs. Vaijanthi.
D. Literature is being taught by Mrs. Vaijanthi to us.

Q.15 Direction: Choose the option that is the passive form of the given sentence.

This bottle contains milk.

A. Milk is contained in this bottle.
B. Milk is contained by this bottle.
C. Milk was contained in this bottle.
D. Milk is contained for this bottle.

Q.16 Direction: Choose the option that is the passive form of the given sentence.

Rabindranath Tagore wrote the 'Gitanjali'.

A. The 'Gitanjali' was written by Rabindranath Tagore.
B. The 'Gitanjali' is written by Rabindranath Tagore.
C. The 'Gitanjali' is being written by Rabindranath Tagore.
D. The 'Gitanjali' has been written by Rabindranath Tagore.

Q.17 Direction: Choose the option that is the active form of the given sentence.

Stamp collection interested the boy.

A. The boy were interested in stamp collection.
B. The boy interested in stamp collection.
C. The boy was interested for stamp collection.
D. The boy was interested in stamp collection.

Q.18 Direction: Choose the option that is the passive form of the given sentence.

He might have taken the wrong turn.

A. The wrong turn might have been taken by him.
B. He might have been taken the wrong turn.
C. The wrong turn might be taken by him.
D. The wrong turn may been taken by him.

Q.19 Direction: Choose the option that is the passive form of the given sentence.

Harsh has applied for leave.

A. Leave had been applied by Harsh.
B. Leave was applied by Harsh.
C. Leave has been applied for by Harsh.
D. Leave is applied for by Harsh.

Ques (20-22):Direction: Choose the option that is the passive form of the given sentence.

Q.20 Let the shops be opened.

A. The shops should be opened.
B. Have the shops opened?
C. Open the shops.
D. The shops are open.

Q.21 My mother gave me an interesting book.

A. An interesting book is given to me by my mother.
B. I am given an interesting book by my mother.
C. I was given an interesting book by my mother.
D. An interesting book has been given to my mother.

Q.22 He asked me to sing a song.

A. I was being asked to sing a song.
B. I was asked to sing a song.
C. I had been asked to sing a song.
D. I am asked to sing a song.

Q.23 Direction: Choose the option that is the active form of the given sentence.

Kites have been bought by many children.

A. Many children have bought kites.
B. Many children bought kites.
C. Many children had bought kites.
D. Many children are buying kites.

Ques (24-26):Direction: Choose the option that is the passive form of the given sentence.

Q.24 Only home-cooked food is eaten by us.

A. We are eating only home-cooked food.
B. We ate only home-cooked food.
C. We eat only home-cooked food.
D. We have eaten only home-cooked food.

Q.25 They are lifting the car with a crane.

A. The car had lifted with a crane.
B. The car is lifted with a crane.
C. The car was being lifted with a crane.
D. The car is being lifted with a crane.

Q.26 They are making elaborate arrangements for the party.

A. Elaborate arrangements have been made for the party.
B. Elaborate arrangements were being made for the party.
C. Elaborate arrangements are made for the party.
D. Elaborate arrangements are being made for the party.

Ques (27-28):Direction: Choose the option that is the active form of the given sentence.

Q.27 This picture had been drawn by me.
[SSC Sub Inspector (CPO), 2018], [SSC Sub Inspector (CPO), 2017]

A. I had drawn this picture.
B. I have drawn this picture.
C. I drew this picture.
D. I drawn this picture.

Q.28 A few bags were bought by me.
[SSC Sub Inspector (CPO), 2018], [SSC Sub Inspector (CPO), 2017]

A. I had bought a few bags.
B. I have bought a few bags.
C. I bought a few bags.
D. I buy a few bags.

Ques (29-30):Direction: Choose the option that is the passive form of the given sentence.

Q.29 Sumanth was reading a book.
[SSC Sub Inspector (CPO), 2018], [SSC Sub Inspector (CPO), 2017]

A. A book was being read by Sumanth.
B. A book is being read by Sumanth.
C. A book is read by Sumanth.
D. A book has been read by Sumanth.

Q.30 My elder brother is playing cricket.

[SSC Sub Inspector (CPO), 2018], [SSC Sub Inspector (CPO), 2017]

A. Cricket was being played by my elder brother.

B. Cricket is being played by my elder brother.

C. Cricket has been played by my elder brother.

D. Cricket had been played by my elder brother.

// Smart Answer Sheet //

Correct Indicates percentage of students who answered questions correctly.

Skipped Indicates percentage of students who skipped questions.

Q.	Ans.	Correct	Skipped
1	B	88.75 %	11.12 %
2	A	84.85 %	12.18 %
3	B	89.54 %	10.03 %
4	A	85.85 %	10.28 %
5	D	83.32 %	13.27 %
6	C	86.95 %	12.64 %
7	C	81.63 %	15.56 %
8	A	80.28 %	14.04 %
9	B	86.05 %	13.92 %
10	C	79.25 %	18.33 %
11	A	76.21 %	20.29 %
12	B	78.6 %	20.37 %
13	B	88.49 %	11.3 %
14	C	83.43 %	10.97 %
15	A	78.12 %	14.24 %
16	A	83.55 %	14.99 %
17	D	77.85 %	11.94 %
18	A	81.8 %	11.74 %
19	C	85.96 %	12.53 %
20	C	81.67 %	10.45 %
21	C	83.15 %	12.32 %
22	B	84.22 %	14.43 %
23	A	84.57 %	15.41 %
24	C	88.53 %	10.39 %
25	D	82.53 %	14.16 %
26	D	82.8 %	12.24 %
27	A	83.28 %	13.38 %
28	C	89.57 %	10.16 %
29	A	77.43 %	10.74 %
30	B	86.46 %	13.49 %

Performance Analysis	
Avg. Score (%)	50.0%
Toppers Score (%)	70.0%
Your Score	

//Hints and Solutions//

1. Active form- 'An arrow hit him in the eye.'

Find the subject (He) and object (An arrow) of the sentence and exchange their places. The given sentence is in the simple past tense. The active verb form for simple past is:

- Subject + past participle form of the verb + object.
- So, 'was hit' changes to 'hit'.

Hence, the correct option is (B).

2. Active form - They might promote you this year.

Active- Subject + modal verb + V_1 + Object.

Example: She might do her task.

Hence, the correct option is (A).

3. Active form- She is composing a new song.

Active form- Subject + is/am/are + V_1 + ing + Object

Follow the active form structure for the present continuous tense given above:

- Exchange the places of the subject and object. (A new song - her)
- Since the given subject 'She' is a singular pronoun, the auxiliary verb 'is' will also be singular.
- Now the present participle form of the verb will be used. (composing)

Hence, the correct option is (B).

4. The above given sentence is in the active voice.

We need to change it in the passive voice.

The following steps are required to change the given sentence into passive voice:-

- The subject 'the child' of the active voice will become the object of the passive voice.
- The object 'the page of the book' of the active voice will become the subject of the passive voice.

The tense(simple past tense) will change according to the following structure:

- Active Voice - Subject + did + V_1 or V_2 (tore) + Object.
- Passive Voice - Object + was/were + V_3 (torn) + by + Object.

Therefore, the correct passive voice is The page of the book was torn by the child.

Hence, the correct option is (A).

5. The above given sentence is in the active voice.

We need to change it into passive voice.

We need to follow the given steps for converting the sentence into passive voice:-

- The subject 'the class teacher' of the active voice becomes the object of the passive voice.
- The object 'the children' of the active voice becomes the subject of the passive voice.

The tense(past continuous tense) will be changed according to the following structure:-

- Active Voice - Subject + was/were + V_{ing} + Object.
- Passive Voice - Object + was/were + being + V_3 + Subject.

Thus, 'was taking' will be replaced by 'were being taken'.

The correct answer is: The children were being taken to the zoo by their class teacher.

Hence, the correct option is (D).

6. In the passive form, the subject and the object will be interchanged. So, 'my hand' will become the subject. The sentence uses the past participle form of the verb i.e., burnt. The passive form will be in the past tense.

Option (A) is in past continuous tense.

Option (B) uses could which should be used only when 'can' is there in the active form.

Option (D) is in future tense.

The correct answer is: My hand was burnt yesterday while cooking.

Hence, the correct option is (C).

7. The above given sentence is in the active voice.

We need to change it in the passive voice.

The following steps are required to change the given sentence into passive voice:

- The subject 'the Municipal Corporation' of the active voice will become the object of the passive voice.
- The object 'the manhole covers' of the active voice will become the subject of the passive voice.

The tense(simple past tense) will change according to the following structure:-

- Active Voice - Subject + did + V_1 or V_2 + Object.
- Passive Voice - Object + was/were + V_3 + by + Object.

Hence, the correct option is (C).

8. The above given sentence is in the passive voice.

We need to change it into an active voice.

We need to follow the given steps for converting the given sentence into active voice:

- In sentences containing 'who', the passive starts with 'by whom'.

The following structure is followed:-

- Active Voice - Who + V_1 + Object?
- Passive Voice - By whom + helping verb + Object + V_3?

Thus, 'written' will be converted to 'wrote'.

Hence, the correct option is (A).

9. The above-given sentence is in the active voice.

We need to change it in the passive voice.

The following steps are required to change the given sentence into passive voice:

- The subject 'the tennis ball' of the active voice will become the object of the passive voice.
- The object 'Dhiraj' of the active voice will become the subject of the passive voice.

The tense(simple past tense) will change according to the following structure:

- Active Voice - Subject + did + V_1 or V_2 + Object.
- Passive Voice - Object + was/were + V_3 + by + Object.

Thus, 'hit' will be converted to 'was hit'.

Hence, the correct option is (B).

10. The correct answer is:

A large fish was caught by the fisherman.

The voice of a verb tells whether the subject of the sentence performs or receives the action.

In active voice, the subject (agent) acts upon the verb; while in passive, the verb acts upon the subject (agent).

Rules of Conversion from Active to Passive Voice:

- Identify the subject, the verb and the object: S+V+O
- Change the object into subject
- Put the suitable helping verb or auxiliary verb
- Change the verb into past participle of the verb
- Add the preposition "by"
- Change the subject into object

Option (C) follows the rules of transformation clearly.

Hence, the correct option is (C).

11. The correct answer is:

"104 more runs are needed for them to win the match."

The sentence in question is in active voice. The principal verb in the sentence is in the simple present tense.

Rules of Conversion from Active to Passive Voice:

- Identify the subject, the verb, and the object: S+V+O
- Change the object into subject
- Add suitable helping verb or auxiliary verb
- Change the main verb into past participle form
- Add the preposition "by" or "for"
- Change the subject into object.

Example:

Active Voice: Sameer wrote a letter. (Subject) + (verb) + (object).

Passive Voice: A letter was written by Sameer. (Object) + (auxiliary verb) + (past participle) + (by subject).

Option (A) follows all the sentence transformation rules correctly.

Hence, the correct option is (A).

12. The voice of a verb tells whether the subject of the sentence performs or receives the action.

- Rules of Conversion from Passive to Active Voice:
- Identify the subject, the verb and the object: S+V+O
- Change the subject into object
- Omit the suitable helping verb or auxiliary verb
- Change the past participle of the verb into its simple form.
- Remove the preposition "by"
- Change the object into subject.

Option (B) only fulfils all the conversion criteria.

The correct answer is: Have you despatched your message?

Hence, the correct option is (B).

13. The given sentence is in the passive voice.

I am sometimes puzzled by her actions.

We need to change it into active voice:

- The subject 'I' becomes the object 'me' of the active voice.
- The object 'her actions' becomes the subject of the active voice.

Simple present tense changes in the following manner:-

- Passive Voice - is/am/are + V_3
- Active Voice - (do/does + V_1) or (V_1 s/es)

Thus, 'am sometimes puzzled' will be converted to 'sometimes puzzle'.

Hence, the correct option is (B).

14. The given sentence is in the active voice. It is a simple form of present tense. The structures for active/passive voices are:

Active: Subject + verb ("s" or "es" with singular noun) + object.

Passive: Object + is/are/am + verb (IIIrd form) + by + subject.

So, based on the above structures, we can convert the given sentence into passive voice:

Literature is taught to us by Mrs. Vaijanthi.

Hence, the correct option is (C).

15. The given sentence is in the active voice. It is a simple to form of present tense. The structures for active/passive voices are:

Active: Subject + verb ("s" or "es" with singular noun) + object

Passive: Object + Is/are/am + verb (IIIrd form) + by + subject

So, based on the above structures, we can convert the given sentence into passive voice:

Milk is contained in this bottle.

Please note that here the verb "contained" will be followed by the preposition "in" and not "by".

Hence, the correct option is (A).

16. The 'Gitanjali' was written by Rabindranath Tagore.

Given sentence is in the simple past tense and it is in active voice, we need to change it into passive voice.

Rule: Subject + (was / were) + V_3 + Optional Agents.

Hence, the correct option is (A).

17. The given sentence is in active form of simple past tense. The structures for active/passive voices are:

Active: Subject + verb (IInd form) + object.

Passive: Object + was/were + verb (IIIrd form) + by + subject.

For the given sentence, the verb "interest" will take the preposition "in" with it in the passive voice.

So, with the help of the above structures, we can convert the given sentence into passive voice:

The boy was interested in stamp collection.

Hence, the correct option is (D).

18. The sentence uses the modal verb "might have" which shows the possibility of something that happened in the past when one is not sure about it. The given sentence is in the passive voice. The structure for active/passive will be:

Active: Subject + might + have + verb (third form) + object.

Passive: Object + might + have + been + verb (third form) + by + subject.

So, the active voice of the given sentence would be:

The wrong turn might have been taken by him.

Hence, the correct option is (A).

19. Find the subject (Harsh) and object (leave) of the sentence and exchange their places. The given sentence is in the present perfect tense. The passive verb form for the present perfect is:

Has/have + been + past participle form of the verb.

So, 'has applied' changes to 'has been applied'.

Passive form- Leave has been applied for by Harsh.

Hence, the correct option is (C).

20. An imperative sentence does not normally have a subject. It is used to express a command or request. The imperative sentence in the active and passive voice takes the following form:

- V_1 + Object.
- Let + object + be + past participle.

Example:

Help him. (Active Voice)

Let him be helped. (Passive Voice)

Active form: Open the shops.

Hence, the correct option is (C).

21. In Passive Voice, a sentence emphasizes the action or the object of the sentence. When we convert this sentence into passive voice, the subject 'My mother' of the active voice becomes the object, the object 'me' becomes the subject 'I'. The passive format "was + V3 (given)" should be used.

Passive form: I was given an interesting book by my mother.

Hence, the correct option is (C).

22. In Passive Voice, a sentence emphasizes the action or the object of the sentence. The given sentence is in the active voice and 'He' is the subject and 'me' is the object.

When we convert this sentence into passive voice, the subject 'He' of the active voice becomes the hidden object 'him', the object 'me' becomes the subject 'I'. The passive format "was + V_3 (asked)" should be used.

Passive form- I was asked to sing a song.

Hence, the correct option is (B).

23. The structure of the given sentence as follows:

Subject+has/have+V_3+Object. (Active Voice)

'Kites' will be put in place of 'many children'. (Subject becomes object)

'Children' will be put in place of 'Kites'. (object becomes subject)

'Have been bought' will be changed into 'have bought'. (present perfect passive tense will change to-infinitive form of the present perfect tense)

Active form: 'Many children have bought kites.'

Hence, the correct option is (A).

24. The structure of the given sentence is as follows:

Subject+Verb+Object. (Active Voice)

'Us' will be changed into 'we'. (because now the noun has become the subject from object)

'Is eaten' will be changed into 'eat'.

Active form: 'We eat only home-cooked food.'

Hence, the correct option is (C).

25. The process of transformation is as follows:

The subject of the given sentence is 'they'. The object of the given sentence is 'the car'. The subject is put in place of the object and the object will be put in place of the subject.

But in this case, the subject 'they' will become hidden in passive voice because the focus is on the crane being lifted and 'them' only serves as a necessary actor in the active voice, which is no more needed in the passive voice.

'Are lifting' will be changed into 'is being lifted'. Because 'the car' is singular, will be followed by a singular helping verb.

'With a crane' will be written as it is.

Passive form: 'The car is being lifted with a crane.'

Hence, the correct option is (D).

26. The process of transformation is as follows:

The subject of the given sentence is 'They'. The object of the given sentence is 'Elaborate'. The subject will be put in place of the object and the object will be put in place of the subject.

'Are making' will be changed into 'are being made'.

However, the subject 'they' will not be used as 'by them' because it becomes the hidden subject here. This is so because here the action is the central focus and the actor can be any unknown/general entity.

Passive form: 'Elaborate arrangements are being made for the party.'

Hence, the correct option is (D).

27. While converting active to passive or vice versa the subject and object are interchanged.

The given sentence is in the passive, past perfect.

Passive voice form of past perfect: subject + had + been + past participle form of the verb + by + object.

Active voice form of past perfect: subject[object of passive] + had + past participle form of the verb + object[subject of passive].

The correct sentence is- I had drawn this picture.

Hence, the correct option is (A).

28. While converting active to passive or vice versa the subject and object are interchanged.

Passive sentences in the simple past tense have the form--subject + was/were + past participle form of the verb + by + object.

Active sentences in the simple past tense have the form--subject [object of passive] + past tense form of the verb + object[subject of passive].

The correct sentence is- I bought a few bags.

Hence, the correct option is (C).

29. While converting active to passive or vice versa the subject and object are interchanged.

Active sentences in the past continuous tense have the form:

Subject + was/were + -ing form of the verb + object.

Passive sentences in the past continuous tense have the form:

Object of the active sentence + was/were + being + past participle form of the verb + by + subject of the active sentence.

The correct sentence is- A book was being read by Sumanth.

Hence, the correct option is (A).

30. While converting active to passive or vice versa the subject and object are interchanged.

The given sentence is an active voice, present continuous tense with the form:

Subject +is/are/am + ing form of verb+ object.

The passive form of it will be:

Subject[object of active voice] +is/are/am + being + past participle of the verb + by + object [subject of active voice].

The correct sentence is- Cricket is being played by my elder brother.

Hence, the correct option is (B).

Ques (1-5):Direction: In the following passage, some of the words have been left out. Read the passage carefully and select the correct answer out of the four alternatives for the given numbers.

Can ___(1)____ work? Many individuals, having learned to exercise and avoid excessive caloric ___(2)___ are controlling their weight. The ____(3)____ of the ___(4)___ burden from the rich to the poor in many Western countries demonstrates that knowledge and the __(5)__ to act upon it are important.

Q.1 Find the appropriate word for (1).

A. Exercise **B.** Prevention
C. Caution **D.** Anything

Q.2 Find the appropriate word for (2).

A. Count **B.** Index **C.** Food **D.** Intake

Q.3 Find the appropriate word for (3).

A. Mark **B.** Distinction
C. Removal **D.** Shift

Q.4 Find the appropriate word for (4).

A. Obesity **B.** Corpulence
C. Physical **D.** Fat

Q.5 Find the appropriate word for (5).

A. Vulnerability **B.** Ability
C. Expertise **D.** Insight

Ques (6-10):Direction: In the following passage, some of the words have been left out. Read the passage carefully and select the correct answer for the given numbers out of the four alternatives.

Even though we're living in 2018, one can't ___(1)___ that there are ___(2)____ restrictions placed on women's behavior. One of which is the struggle of having a child and _____(3)_____, having a successful career because our society believes that motherhood is a ____(4)____ when it comes to having a career; not for a man, but, ___(5)___ for a woman.

Q.6 Find the appropriate word for (1).

A. Accept **B.** Deny **C.** See **D.** Foresee

Q.7 Find the appropriate word for (2).

A. Some **B.** Any **C.** Certain **D.** All

Q.8 Find the appropriate word for (3).

A. Yet **B.** Though **C.** But **D.** Already

Q.9 Find the appropriate word for (4).

A. Gift **B.** Boon **C.** Difficult **D.** Hurdle

Q.10 Find the appropriate word for (5).

A. Surely **B.** Definitely
C. Must **D.** Absolutely

Ques (11-15):Direction: In the following passage, some words have been deleted. Fill in the blanks with the help of the alternatives given. Select the most appropriate option for each blank.

Ram Singh whistled cheerfully as he pushed his bicycle up the hill towards old Mrs. Gupta's house. His work for the (1)_____was almost finished (2)_____his bag, which was usually (3)_____ when he started from the post office (4)_____now become empty (5)_____for the letter that he had to deliver Mrs.Gupta.

Q.11 Select the most appropriate option to fill in blank no. (1). ***[SSC Sub Inspector (CPO), 2019]***

A. month **B.** day **C.** year **D.** week

Q.12 Select the most appropriate option to fill in blank no. (2). ***[SSC Sub Inspector (CPO), 2019]***

A. although **B.** but **C.** and **D.** unless

Q.13 Select the most appropriate option to fill in blank no. (3). ***[SSC Sub Inspector (CPO), 2019]***

A. large **B.** dirty **C.** torn **D.** heavy

Q.14 Select the most appropriate option to fill in blank no. (4). ***[SSC Sub Inspector (CPO), 2019]***

A. had **B.** have **C.** were **D.** has

Q.15 Select the most appropriate option to fill in blank no. (5). ***[SSC Sub Inspector (CPO), 2019]***

A. excluding **B.** without
C. except **D.** accept

Ques (16-20):Direction: In the following passage some words have been deleted. Fill in the blanks with the help of the alternatives given. Select the most appropriate option for each number.

Alfred Hitchcock was a man with vivid imagination, (1)_____ skills and a passion for life. With his (2)_____ style and God-gifted wit he produced and directed (3)_____ of the most thrilling films that had the audience swooning (4)_____ fright and falling off their seats with laughter. He was greatly (5)_____ by American films and magazines.

Q.16 Select the most appropriate option to fill in blank no (1).

A. leading **B.** original **C.** creative **D.** clever

Q.17 Select the most appropriate option to fill in blank no (2).

A. separate **B.** dull **C.** unique **D.** ordinary

Q.18 Select the most appropriate option to fill in blank no (3).

A. more **B.** some **C.** much **D.** any

Q.19 Select the most appropriate option to fill in blank no (4).

A. through **B.** with **C.** by **D.** of

Q.20 Select the most appropriate option to fill in blank no (5).

A. determined **B.** altered
C. influenced **D.** attached

Ques (21-25):Direction: In the following passage, some words have been deleted. Fill in the blanks with the help of the alternatives given. Select the most appropriate option for each number.

Malti had to wait long to see her son, Abhik. She had worked hard to (1)_____ her husband's last wish that Abhik should (2)_____ his higher education at Cambridge. Abhik (3)_____ to be meritorious and hardworking and had secured a seat. Making ends meet was (4)_____ and a trip back home in the vacation, (5)_____ for the mother and son.

Q.21 Select the most appropriate option to fill in blank no (1).

A. fulfil **B.** finish **C.** produce **D.** perform

Q.22 Select the most appropriate option to fill in blank no (2).

A. provide **B.** pursue **C.** delete **D.** approach

Q.23 Select the most appropriate option to fill in blank no (3).

A. prove **B.** will prove
C. is proving **D.** had proved

Q.24 Select the most appropriate option to fill in blank no (4).

A. inspiring **B.** worthy **C.** difficult **D.** severe

Q.25 Select the most appropriate option to fill in blank no (5).

A. uncouth **B.** unaffordable
C. unbearable **D.** uncomfortable

Ques (26-30):Direction: In the following passage some words have been deleted. Fill in the blanks with the help of the alternatives given. Select the most appropriate option for each number.

Those of us who live in (1) ______ covered with forests and surrounded (2) _____ hills may find it difficult to (3) _____ what a desert is really like. The (4) _____ belief is that it is (5) ______ endless stretch of sand where no rain falls and, therefore. no vegetation grows.

Q.26 Select the most appropriate option that will fill in the blank number (1).

A. quarters **B.** territory **C.** regions **D.** cities

Q.27 Select the most appropriate option that will fill in the blank number (2).

A. by **B.** for **C.** from **D.** with

Q.28 Select the most appropriate option that will fill in the blank number (3).

A. feel **B.** imagine **C.** look **D.** calculate

Q.29 Select the most appropriate option that will fill in the blank number (4).

A. popular **B.** fake
C. attractive **D.** noted

Q.30 Select the most appropriate option that will fill in the blank number (5).

A. the **B.** a
C. no article needed **D.** an

// Smart Answer Sheet //

Correct Indicates percentage of students who answered questions correctly.

Skipped Indicates percentage of students who skipped questions.

Q.	Ans.	Correct	Skipped
1	B	77.15 %	13.58 %
2	D	80.52 %	15.3 %
3	D	77.42 %	13.02 %
4	A	78.84 %	12.4 %
5	B	76.05 %	11.83 %
6	B	89.3 %	10.62 %
7	C	83.89 %	10.16 %
8	A	89.56 %	10.37 %
9	D	89.23 %	10.1 %
10	B	81.49 %	10.29 %
11	B	85.32 %	12.3 %
12	C	87.44 %	12.18 %
13	D	77.01 %	16.73 %
14	A	89.52 %	10.11 %
15	C	82.55 %	12.98 %
16	C	78.94 %	14.51 %
17	C	79.38 %	19.83 %
18	B	86.22 %	10.59 %
19	B	82.33 %	14.58 %
20	C	84.78 %	13.53 %
21	A	89.6 %	10.13 %
22	B	76.77 %	16.7 %
23	D	84.65 %	13.17 %
24	C	88.32 %	11.21 %
25	B	86.5 %	13.17 %
26	C	76.53 %	22.25 %
27	A	86.48 %	11.38 %
28	B	86.07 %	10.97 %
29	A	76.42 %	14.18 %
30	D	82.13 %	14.66 %

Performance Analysis	
Avg. Score (%)	66.67%
Toppers Score (%)	70.0%
Your Score	

//Hints and Solutions//

1. Prevention means the action of stopping something from happening or arising.

Exercise means activity requiring physical effort, carried out to sustain or improve health and fitness.

Caution means care taken to avoid danger or mistakes.

Anything means used to refer to a thing, no matter what.

'Can' implies that we are talking about the capability of the word to be placed in the blank. Also, this word has to 'work'. Generally, 'exercise' and 'anything' are capable doing their job. Also, 'caution' is merely practiced. It doesn't give any results. The sentence is asking whether it is capable of giving results. 'prevention' can do that.

Hence, the correct option is (B).

2. Intake means an amount of food, air, or another substance taken into the body.

Count means to determine the total number of (a collection of items).

Index means a set of items each of which specifies one of the records of a file and contains information about its address.

Food means any nutritious substance that people or animals eat or drink or that plants absorb in order to maintain life and growth.

'Calorie' is a unit of energy. 'caloric' is an adjective that would fit with any of the given options. But the only one that would affect 'weight control' is the calorie that we consume. Food with high calories wouldn't affect us until we consume it.

Hence, the correct option is (D).

3. The shift means to change the emphasis, direction, or focus.

Mark means a line, figure, or symbol made as an indication or record of something.

Distinction means a difference or contrast between similar things or people.

Removal means the action of taking away or abolishing something unwanted.

'burden' is either shifted or removed. But, since we see a change in position (from rich to poor), the burden is being shifted.

Hence, the correct option is (D).

4. Obesity means the state of being grossly fat or overweight.

Corpulence means the state of being fat; obesity.

Physical means relating to the body as opposed to the mind.

Fat means (of a person or animal) having a large amount of excess flesh.

The blank requires a word that would provide additional information about what kind of burden we are talking about. Since the topic of the paragraph is obesity, both obesity and corpulence would ft. but, we have to select the most appropriate word which obesity is because corpulence is rarely used in day to day vernacular these days.

Hence, the correct option is (A).

5. Ability means possession of the means or skill to do something.

Vulnerability means the quality or state of being exposed to the possibility of being attacked or harmed, either physically or emotionally.

Expertise means expert skill or knowledge in a particular field.

Insight means the capacity to gain an accurate and deep understanding of someone or something.

The 'to' following the blank is indicating towards something. The only option for which such directional or indication is necessary is ability. Whenever 'ability' is mentioned, we also have to mention, ability to do what.

Hence, the correct option is (B).

6. Deny means declare untrue; contradict.

Accept means consider or hold as true.

See means perceive by sight or have the power to perceive by sight.

Foresee means realize beforehand.

Restrictions are already present. Something that is already present cannot be denied.

From the above alternatives, we can conclude that deny is the word best suited for blank 1.

Hence, the correct answer is (B).

7. Certain is another word for confident. It is something you know you are right about. Some is a word pertaining to quantity. Usually used when you do not know the exact quantity of things. "any" and "some" basically have the same meaning, but are used in different kinds of sentences. "Any" is used in "negative" statements, sentences that use the word "not". Restrictions are particular. So, all is a wrong choice.

Hence, the correct option is (C).

8. Yet is used when something didn't take place at the time when it was expected. But is used when two contradicting information is present, which is not in the given case.. Already is just the opposite of yet. It shows something happened sooner than it was expected. Tough when used at the end of the sentence, is an adverb that gives the sense of 'despite that'.

Hence, the correct option is (A).

9. Hurdle means an obstacle that you are expected to overcome.

Gift means something acquired without compensation.

Boon means a desirable state.

Difficult means not easy; requiring great physical or mental effort to accomplish or comprehend or endure.

Motherhood is called a struggle in career by our society. It is considered a hurdle.

From the above alternatives, we can conclude that hurdle is the word best suited for blank 4.

Hence, the correct option is (D).

10. Definitely means without question and beyond doubt.

Surely means definitely or positively (`sure' is sometimes used informally for `surely').

Must means a necessary or essential thing.

Absolutely means completely and without qualification; used informally as intensifiers.

From the above alternatives, we can conclude that definitely is the word best suited for blank 5.

Hence, the correct option is (B).

11. Day is the most appropriate option to fill in blank no. (1).

It is clear from the passage that the author is talking about a particular day.

The sentence will be:

Ram Singh was whistling cheerfully as the work allotted to him for that day was finished.

Hence, the correct option is (B).

12. "and" is the most appropriate option to fill in blank no. (2).

And is used to join similar words or sentences.

Although means in spite of the fact.

But is used to introduce a contradicting statement.

Unless means except if; if not.

In this sentence, the author is talking about his work and his bag and is combining two sentences. So, 'and' should be used.

Hence, the correct option is (C).

13. "heavy" is the most appropriate option to fill in blank no. (3).

In the next sentence, the author has said that the bag became empty which means that when he started from the post office the bag must have been heavy.

There is no mention of the size or cleanliness of the bag.

The word 'heavy' means weighing a lot; difficult to lift or move.

Large : greater in size, amount, etc. than usual; big.

Dirty : not clean.

Torn : pull (something) apart or to pieces with force.

Hence, the correct option is (D).

14. "had" is the most appropriate option to fill in blank no. (4).

The sentence uses the past participle form of the verb i.e., started. So, the sentence is in past tense.

Have is used in the present tense.

Example- "I have only six nails," he said, "and it will take a little time to hammer out ten more."

Were is used with plural nouns and bag is singular.

Example- My parents were deeply grieved and perplexed.

Has is used in present tense with pronouns like he/she/it.

Example- If Len has time, maybe he could help me.

Hence, the correct option is (A).

15. "except" is the most appropriate option to fill in blank no. (5).

'Except' should be used as the author is saying that the bag was empty other than the fact that it contained a letter for Mrs. Gupta.

Excluding means except but it is used in the present tense. The sentence is in the past tense.

Without means in the absence of. Example: He lives without his parents.

Except means not including; other than. Example: He likes to eat all fruits except apples.

Accept means consent to receive or undertake (something offered). Example: The Job offer was accepted by her.

Hence, the correct option is (C).

16. The most appropriate word in blank no (1) will be creative.

Alfred Hitchcock was a man with vivid imagination, creative skills and a passion for life.

Creative- relating to or involving the imagination or original ideas, especially in the production of an artistic work

Hence, the correct option is (C).

17. The most appropriate word in blank no (2) will be unique.

With his unique style and God-gifted wit he produced...

Unique- being the only one of its kind; unlike anything else.

Hence, the correct option is (C).

18. The most appropriate word in blank no (3) will be some.

Directed some of the most thrilling films that had the audience swooning...

Some- an unspecified amount or number of.

Hence, the correct option is (B).

19. The most appropriate word in blank no (4) will be with.

With fright and falling off their seats with laughter.

The given phrase 'swoon with' means to feel a lot of pleasure, love, etc. because of something or someone.

Hence, the correct option is (B).

20. The most appropriate word in blank no (5) will be influenced.

He was greatly influenced by American films and magazines.

Influenced- have an influence on

Hence, the correct option is (C).

21. The most appropriate word in blank no (1) will be fulfil.

Malti had to wait long to see her son, Abhik. She had worked hard to fulfil her husband's last wish..

'Fulfil' means to achieve or realize something desired, promised, or predicted.

Hence, the correct option is (A).

22. The most appropriate word in blank no (2) will be pursue.

Abhik should pursue his higher education at Cambridge.

'Pursue' means to seek to attain or accomplish a goal over a long period.

Hence, the correct option is (B).

23. The most appropriate word in blank no (3) will be had proved.

Abhik had proved to be meritorious and hardworking and had secured a seat.

'Had proved' is in the past perfect tense.

Hence, the correct option is (D).

24. The most appropriate word in blank no (4) will be difficult.

Making ends meet was difficult and a trip back home.

'Difficult' means needing much effort or skill to accomplish, deal with or understand.

Hence, the correct option is (C).

25. The most appropriate word in blank no (5) will be unaffordable.

In the vacation, unaffordable for the mother and son.

'Unaffordable' means too expensive to be afforded by the average person.

Hence, the correct option is (B).

26. The most appropriate word in blank no (1) will be regions.

Those of us who live in regions covered with forests.

The word 'regions' means "a particular area or part of the world, or any of the large official areas into which a country is divided".

Example: There's a shortage of cheap housing in the region.

Hence, the correct option is (C).

27. The most appropriate word in blank no (2) will be by.

Forests and surrounded by hills may find it difficult.

by: to show the person or thing that does or signifies something.

Ex: I felt frightened by the anger in his voice.

Hence, the correct option is (A).

28. The most appropriate word in blank no (3) will be imagine.

Imagine what a desert is really like.

Imagine: to form or have a mental picture or idea of something.

Ex: Imagine Robert Redford when he was young - that's what John looks like.

Hence, the correct option is (B).

29. The most appropriate word in blank no (4) will be popular.

The popular belief is that it is....

Popular: liked, enjoyed, or supported by many people.

Ex: She's the most popular teacher in school.

Hence, the correct option is (A).

30. The most appropriate word in blank no (5) will be an.

The popular belief is that it is an endless stretch of sand where no rain falls and, therefore. no vegetation grows.

The indefinite article "an" is used before a singular noun beginning with a vowel sound.

Here, in the given question 'endless' is beginning with a vowel sound.

Hence, the correct option is (D).

Q.1 Direction: Select the correct indirect form of the given sentence.

The teacher says, "Magnets attract objects made of iron."

[SSC CGL, 2020]

A. The teacher says magnets attracts objects made of iron.
B. The teacher says that magnets attract objects made of iron.
C. The teacher said that magnets attracted objects made of iron.
D. The teacher said that magnets were attracting objects made of iron.

Q.2 Direction: Select the correct indirect form of the given sentence.

The Prime Minister has said, "The government will extend help to the unorganised sector."

[SSC CGL, 2020]

A. The Prime Minister said that the government has extended help to the unorganised sector.
B. The Prime Minister said that the government would extend help to the unorganised sector.
C. The Prime Minister has said that the government will extend help to the unorganised sector.
D. The Prime Minister has said that the government extended help to the unorganised sector.

Q.3 Direction: Select the correct direct form of the given sentence.

The boy requested his mother to give him a mango.

[SSC CGL, 2020]

A. The boy said to his mother, "Give me a mango now."
B. The mother said to the boy, "Give him a mango."
C. The boy said to his mother, "Will you give me a mango?"
D. The boy said to his mother, "Please give me a mango."

Q.4 Direction: Select the correct indirect form of the given sentence.

Mother said to her, "Paint the river blue."

[SSC CGL, 2020]

A. Mother told to her paint the river blue.
B. Mother asked her paint the river blue.
C. Mother said her to paint the river blue.
D. Mother told her to paint the river blue.

Q.5 Directions: Select the correct direct form of the given sentence.

He asked me if I would like to learn French.

[SSC CGL, 2020]

A. He said to me, "You would like to learn French?"
B. He said to me, "I would like to learn French."
C. He said to me, "Do you like to learn French?"
D. He said to me, "Would you like to learn French?"

Q.6 Directions: Select the correct direct form of the given sentence.

"Come out from where you are hiding." shouted the police at the suspect.

A. The police shouted at the suspect to come out from where he was hiding.
B. The police shouted at the suspect to come out from where he is hiding.
C. The police shouts at the suspect to come out from where he was hiding.
D. The police shouts at the suspect to come out from where he is hiding.

Q.7 Directions: Select the correct indirect form of the given sentence.

He said to his brother, "Pack your bags and leave now."

[SSC CGL, 2020]

A. He told his brother that pack your bags and leave now.
B. He suggested his brother that he should pack his bags and leave then.
C. He instructed his brother to pack his bags and leave then.
D. He ordered his brother to pack your bags and leave now.

Q.8 Direction: Select the correct direct form of the given sentence.

She told her brother that she was going to meet her friend.

[SSC CGL, 2020]

A. She said to her brother, "She will go to meet her friend."
B. She said to her brother, "I am gone to meet her friend."
C. She said to her brother, "I was going to meet my friend."
D. She said to her brother, "I am going to meet my friend."

Q.9 Direction: Select the correct indirect form of the given sentence.

She said to me, "Have you ever flown a kite?"

[SSC CGL, 2020]

A. She asked me if I ever flew a kite.
B. She asked me that had I ever flown a kite.
C. She asked me if I had ever flown a kite.
D. She asked me if you have ever flown a kite.

Q.10 Direction: Select the correct indirect form of the given sentence.

He said to Manoj, "I celebrated my birthday two days ago."

[SSC CGL, 2020]

A. He told Manoj that he celebrated my birthday two days before.
B. He told Manoj that he had celebrated his birthday two days before.
C. He told Manoj that he celebrated his birthday two days ago.
D. He told Manoj that I celebrated my birthday two days ago.

Q.11 Direction: Select the correct indirect form of the given sentence.

The librarian said to her, "You can borrow only two books at a time."

[SSC CGL, 2020]

A. The librarian told her that she could borrow only two books at a time.
B. The librarian told her that she can borrow only two books at a time.
C. The librarian told her that you can borrow only two books at a time.
D. The librarian told her that they could borrow only two books at a time.

Q.12 Direction: Select the correct indirect form of the given sentence.

The Principal says, "Hard work is the key to success."

[SSC CGL, 2020]

A. The Principal said that hard work was the key to success.
B. The Principal says that hard work was the key to success.
C. The Principal says that hard work is the key to success.
D. The Principal say that hard work is the key to success.

Q.13 Direction: Select the correct indirect form of the given sentence.

He said to me, "Your father is waiting for you at the reception."

[SSC CGL, 2020]

A. He told me that your father was waiting for him at the reception.
B. He told me that my father was waiting for me at the reception.
C. He told me that his father was waiting for you at the reception.
D. He told to me my father was waiting for you at the reception.

Q.14 Choose the option that is the indirect form of the sentence.

Akshay said, "I am making biryani today."

[SSC Sub Inspector (CPO), 2019]

A. Akshay said that he made biryani today.
B. Akshay said that he would be making biryani on the next day.
C. Akshay said that he is making biryani today.
D. Akshay said that he was making biryani on that day.

Q.15 Choose the option that is the indirect form of the sentence.

Jaya told me "I've been waiting for you since 4 pm."

[SSC Sub Inspector (CPO), 2019]

A. Jaya told me that she had been waiting for me since 4 pm.
B. Jaya told me that she will be waiting for me since 4 pm.
C. Jaya told me she was waiting for you since 4 pm.
D. Jaya said me that she has been waiting for me since 4 pm.

Q.16 Choose the option that is the direct form of the sentence.

I told them to be quiet.

[SSC Sub Inspector (CPO), 2019]

A. I said to them "Be you quiet!"
B. I told to them, "You must be quiet."
C. I said to them, "Be quiet!"
D. I said them, "You be quiet."

Q.17 Choose the option that is the indirect form of the sentence.

The judge said to Jia, "Stand in the witness box."

[SSC Sub Inspector (CPO), 2019]

A. The judge told Jia you are standing in the witness box.
B. The judge told Jia to stand in the witness box.
C. The judge told to Jia stand in the witness box.
D. The judge told Jia you will stand in the witness box.

Q.18 Choose the option that is the indirect form of the sentence.

"I'm hungry" said the child to his mother.

[SSC Sub Inspector (CPO), 2019]

A. The child said his mother that he is hungry.
B. The child said to his mother that I am hungry.
C. The child told his mother that she was hungry.
D. The child told his mother that he was hungry.

Q.19 Direction: In the following question, a sentence has been given in Direct/Indirect Speech. Out of the four alternatives suggested, select the one which best expresses the same sentence in Indirect/Direct Speech.

The priest said, "December is the last month of the year".

A. The priest said that December was the last month of the year
B. The priest said that December is the last month of the year
C. The priest says that December is the last month of the year
D. The priest told that December is the last month of the year

Q.20 Direction: Rewrite the sentence in the direct speech.

Sumanth said that he would have called a doctor.

A. Sumanth said, "I will call a doctor"
B. Sumanth said, "I will be calling a doctor"
C. Sumanth said, "I will have called a doctor"
D. Sumanth said, "I should call a doctor"

Q.21 Direction: Rewrite the sentence in the direct speech.

Anjana said that she was waiting for her friends.

A. Anjana said, "I have been waiting for my friends"
B. Anjana said, "I had been waiting for my friends"
C. Anjana said, "I waiting for my friends"
D. Anjana said, "I am waiting for my friends"

Q.22 Direction: Rewrite the sentence in the indirect speech.

Kumar said, "I am unwell."

A. Kumar said that he had been unwell.
B. Kumar said that he is unwell.
C. Kumar said that he has been unwell.
D. Kumar said that he was unwell.

Q.23 Direction: Rewrite the sentence in the indirect speech.

Anbu said to Suresh, "Priya is playing in the garden."

A. Anbu told Suresh that Priya was playing in the garden.

B. Anbu told Suresh that Priya played in the garden.
C. Anbu told Suresh that Priya plays in the garden.
D. Anbu told Suresh that Priya play in the garden.

Q.24 Direction: Rewrite the sentence in the indirect speech.
Vasanth said to Praveen, "I have eaten three apples."
A. Vasanth told Praveen that he ate three apples.
B. Vasanth told Praveen that he has eaten three apples.
C. Vasanth told Praveen that he had eaten three apples.
D. Vasanth told Praveen that he eats three apples.

Q.25 Direction: Rewrite the sentence in the indirect speech.
Anitha said, "I've been learning Bharatanatyam for the past six months."
A. Anitha said that she had been learning Bharatanatyam for the past six months.
B. Anitha said that she has been learning Bharatanatyam for the past six months.
C. Anitha said that she is learning Bharatanatyam for the past six months.
D. Anitha said that she learnt Bharatanatyam for the past six months.

Q.26 Direction: Rewrite the sentence in the indirect speech.
Sunder said, "I will go to my sister's house today."
A. Sunder said that he went to his sister's house that day.
B. Sunder said that he has to go to his sister's house that day.
C. Sunder said that he goes to his sister's house that day.
D. Sunder said that he would go to his sister's house that day.

Q.27 Direction: Rewrite the sentence in the indirect speech.
Nisha said to Sunil, "I will not be going for the class."
A. Nisha told Sunil that she will not have gone for the class.
B. Nisha told Sunil that she does not go for the class.
C. Nisha told Sunil that she would not be going for the class.
D. Nisha told Sunil that she had not been going for the class.

Q.28 Direction: Rewrite the sentence in the indirect speech.
"Where do you live?", said the stranger.
A. The stranger enquired where I lived.
B. The stranger enquires where I lived.
C. The stranger enquired where I had been living.
D. The stranger enquires where I have been living.

Q.29 Direction: Rewrite the sentence in the indirect speech.
"Call the first witness," said the judge.
A. The judge commands to call the first witness.
B. The judge pleaded to call the first witness.
C. The judge commanded to called the first witness.
D. The judge commanded to call the first witness.

Q.30 Direction: Rewrite the sentence in the indirect speech.
Siva said, "I have read the novel Pride and Prejudice."
A. Siva said that he have read the novel Pride and Prejudice.
B. Siva said that he reads the novel Pride and Prejudice.
C. Siva said that he had read the novel Pride and Prejudice.
D. Siva said that he read the novel Pride and Prejudice.

// Smart Answer Sheet //

Correct Indicates percentage of students who answered questions correctly.

Skipped Indicates percentage of students who skipped questions.

Q.	Ans.	Correct	Skipped
1	B	80.46 %	15.78 %
2	C	85.25 %	13.84 %
3	D	87.15 %	11.81 %
4	D	88.15 %	11.73 %
5	D	79.83 %	13.69 %
6	B	81.67 %	12.46 %

Q.	Ans.	Correct	Skipped
7	C	82.98 %	12.5 %
8	D	82.82 %	12.7 %
9	C	86.76 %	11.51 %
10	B	89.48 %	10.2 %
11	A	76.77 %	19.79 %
12	C	84.94 %	14.37 %

Q.	Ans.	Correct	Skipped
13	B	86.18 %	11.73 %
14	D	77.75 %	21.39 %
15	A	80.04 %	10.13 %
16	C	89.88 %	10.12 %
17	B	82.98 %	13.65 %
18	D	81.35 %	16.13 %

Q.	Ans.	Correct	Skipped
19	B	86.9 %	10.19 %
20	C	81.57 %	16.29 %
21	D	81.74 %	16.32 %
22	D	77.4 %	19.16 %
23	A	79.91 %	12.77 %
24	C	87.55 %	12.05 %

Q.	Ans.	Correct	Skipped
25	A	84.89 %	14.03 %
26	D	78.98 %	20.64 %
27	C	83.67 %	15.83 %
28	A	87.03 %	12.9 %
29	D	85.0 %	12.44 %
30	C	81.95 %	17.25 %

Performance Analysis	
Avg. Score (%)	36.67%
Toppers Score (%)	70.0%
Your Score	

//Hints and Solutions//

1. Indirect form- The teacher says that magnets attract objects made of iron.

When the indirect speech is in an assertive form, we follow the steps given below:

- The reporting verb says will remain the same as no object is mentioned after it.
- Connectors 'that' is replaced by a comma and inverted commas.
- The tense of indirect/reported speech will remain the same as the reporting verb (says) is in the present tense.

Hence, the correct option is (B).

2. Indirect form - The Prime Minister has said that the government will extend help to the unorganised sector.

When the indirect speech is in an assertive form, we follow the steps given below:

- The reporting verb has said will remain the same as no object is mentioned after it.
- Connector 'that' will replace the comma and inverted commas.
- The tense of indirect/reported speech will remain the same as the reporting verb(has said) is in the present tense.

Hence, the correct option is (C).

3. Direct form- The boy said to his mother, "Please give me a mango."

When the direct speech is in an imperative form, we follow the steps given below:

- Change the sentence in the direct speech from imperative to assertive.
- The tense of reported speech is changed only when the reporting verb is in the past tense.
- The reporting verb said to will replace requested.
- 'To infinitive' is replaced by a comma and inverted commas followed by the word 'please'.
- 'to give' changes into 'give'.
- Similarly 'him' changes into 'me'.

Hence, the correct option is (D).

4. Indirect form- Mother told her to paint the river blue.

When the direct speech is in an imperative form, we follow the steps given below:

- Change the sentence in direct speech from imperative to assertive.
- The tense of reported speech is changed only when the reporting verb is in the past tense.
- The reporting verb said to is converted into told.
- 'To infinitive' is used in place of comma and inverted commas followed by the 1st form of the verb.
- 'paint' changes into 'to paint'.

Hence, the correct option is (D).

5. Direct form- He said to me, "Would you like to learn French?"

Basic rules for changing or converting indirect speech into direct speech:

- The commas, inverted commas, and the exclamation mark are added.
- In the first part of the sentence, the verb "asked" will be changed to "said" in the direct speech.
- The first person 'I' will be changed into the second person 'you'.
- A reported question (?) is when we tell someone what another person asked.
- The modal verbs "might, could, would, should, ought to" do not change in reported speech.

Hence, the correct option is (D).

6. The basic rules for changing or converting direct speech into indirect speech:

- Remove comma and inverted commas.
- The conjunction 'that' is used in place of commas and inverted commas.

Here, the direct speech is in the present continuous tense (Subject +is/am/are+V1 +ing+ Object), thus we have to change it into the corresponding past continuous tense (Subject +was/were+V1 +ing+ Object) in the indirect speech.

Also, the pronoun "you" in "direct speech" is changed into 'he' in "indirect speech".

From the following rules, we get the correct sentence as "The police shouted at the suspect to come out from where he was hiding."

Hence, the correct option is (A).

7. Indirect form- He instructed his brother to pack his bags and leave then.

The basic rules for changing or converting direct speech into indirect speech:

- The commas, inverted commas, and the questions mark are removed and "to-infinitive" should be used.
- The reporting verb 'instructed' should be used in place of 'said' as instruction is given to the brother.
- The second person pronoun 'your' should be converted into the third person pronoun 'his'.
- The adverb 'now' should be converted into 'then'.

Hence, the correct option is (C).

8. Direct form- She said to her brother, "I am going to meet my friend."

The basic rules for changing or converting indirect speech into direct speech:

- 'Told' will be changed into 'said to'.
- Comma and Inverted commas will be added.
- 'She' will be changed into 'I'.
- 'Was going' will be changed into 'am going'.

Hence, the correct option is (D).

9. Indirect form- 'She asked me if I had ever flown a kite.'

The basic rules for changing or converting direct speech into indirect speech:

- The given question is an example of an Interrogative sentence.
- 'Said to' will be changed into 'asked'.
- 'If' conjunction will be added to represent whether something is true or not
- 'You' will be changed into 'I'. (Second person->First person)
- 'Have' will be changed into 'had' (Present perfect tense-Past Perfect tense)

Hence, the correct option is (C).

10. Indirect form- 'He told Manoj that he had celebrated his birthday two days before.'

The basic rules for changing or converting direct speech into indirect speech:

- 'Said to' will be changed into 'told'.
- 'That' conjunction will be added to account for the comma and double-inverted commas (starting a direct speech)
- 'I' will be changed into 'he'. (first-person -> third-person)
- 'Celebrated' will be changed into 'Had celebrated'. (simple past to past perfect)
- 'My' will be changed into 'his'. (first-person -> third-person)
- 'Ago' will be changed into 'before'.

Hence, the correct option is (B).

11. Indirect form- 'The librarian told her that she could borrow only two books at a time.'

The basic rules for changing or converting direct speech into indirect speech:

- 'Said to' will be changed into 'told'.
- 'That' conjunction will be added.
- 'You' will be changed into 'She'. (Second-person -> Third-person)
- 'Can' will be changed into 'could'. (Direct to Indirect form)

Hence, the correct option is (A).

12. Indirect form- 'The Principal says that hard work is the key to success.'

The process of transformation is as follows:

- In the given sentence Reporting Verb is in the present tense. Therefore, there will be no change in the Reported Speech.
- The given sentence is a universal truth as well. We know that when Universal Truth, Proverb, Habitual truth, Historical event in the past, etc. is used as a Reported Speech their tense does not change.
- Only the comma and double quotes will be replaced with 'that'

Hence, the correct option is (C).

13. Indirect form- 'He told me that my father was waiting for me at the reception.'

The process of transformation is as follows:

- 'Said to' will be changed into 'told'. (Direct form to Indirect form)
- 'That' conjunction will be added to convert to Indirect form.
- 'Your' will be changed into 'my'. (Second-person -> First-person)
- 'Is waiting' will be changed into 'was waiting'. (Present continuous to Past continuous)
- 'You' will be changed into 'me'. (Second-person -> First-person)

Hence, the correct option is (B).

14. The correct answer is:

Akshay said that he was making biryani on that day.

The given sentence is in present continuous tense (am making) so the indirect form will be in past continuous tense (was making).

The first person 'I' will be changed to third person 'He'.

The only option which follows the structure (past continuous tense) is Option (D).

Option (A) is in simple past tense (made).

Option (B) is in future perfect continuous tense (would be making).

Option (C) is in present continuous tense (is making).

Hence, the correct option is (D).

15. The correct answer of the given direct form is:

"Jaya told me that she had been waiting for me since 4 pm."

The given sentence is in present perfect continuous tense so the indirect form will be in past perfect continuous tense.

The first person 'I' changes to third person 'she'.

Thus, the option which follows the correct structure (past perfect continuous) is option (A).

Option (B) is in future continuous tense (will be waiting).

Option (C) is in past continuous tense (was waiting).

Option (D) is in present perfect continuous tense (has been waiting).

Hence, the correct option is (A).

16. The correct answer is:

I said to them, "Be quiet!".

The given sentence is an order given by the speaker. In the direct form, it will be simple transformed to "Be quiet!".

All the other options are incorrect as they use 'you' which is incorrect as the speaker is not referring to a particular person.

Hence, the correct option is (C).

17. The correct answer is:

"The judge told Jia to stand in the witness box."

The sentence is in the simple present tense. So the indirect form will be in the present tense.

Option (A) is in the present continuous tense.

Option (C) is incorrect as the preposition 'to' is incorrectly used.

Option (D) is incorrect as the second person pronoun 'you' cannot be used in the indirect form.

Hence, the correct option is (B).

18. The correct answer is:

The child told his mother that he was hungry.

The child is telling something to his mother. So, 'told' should be used. We are left with option (C) and (D). The statement is in simple present tense, so the indirect form will be in simple past tense. Also, in the sentence 'his' is used which means the child is a male.

Hence, the correct option is (D).

19.

- In affirmative sentences, the Reporting verb 'said' in 'direct sentence' is written as it is in 'indirect sentence' i.e. 'said' in indirect speech.
- 'that' is written in place of 'inverted commas'.
- In the case of universal truth/ general fact/ accepted beliefs, the tense in indirect speech is the same as that of direct speech.

The correct sentence is: The priest said that December is the last month of the year.

Hence, the correct option is (B).

20. Sumanth said, "I will have called a doctor"

While changing a sentence from indirect speech to direct speech, we need to follow these steps-

- The conjunction 'that' will be replaced with a comma (,) and inverted commas (" ").
- 'Said' remains unchanged.
- 'Would' is changed into 'will'.
- The third-person 'he' is changed into the first-person 'I' i.e. according to the subject of the reporting verb. (Sumanth)

Hence, the correct option is (C).

21. Anjana said, "I am waiting for my friends"

While changing a sentence from indirect speech to direct speech, we need to follow these steps-

- The conjunction 'that' will be replaced with a comma (,) and inverted commas (" ").
- 'Said' remains unchanged.
- The past continuous tense (was waiting) is changed into the present continuous tense (am waiting).
- The third-person 'she' is changed into the first-person 'I' i.e. according to the subject of the reporting verb. (Anjana)

Hence, the correct option is (D).

22. Kumar said that he was unwell.

While changing the narration of an assertive sentence, we need to follow the given steps-

- The conjunction 'that' should be used in place of a comma (,) and inverted commas (" ").
- 'Said' remains unchanged.
- The simple present tense (am) is changed into the simple past tense (was).
- The first-person (I) is changed into the third-person (he) i.e. subject of the reporting verb. (Kumar)

Hence, the correct option is (D).

23. Anbu told Suresh that Priya was playing in the garden.

While changing the narration of an assertive sentence, we need to follow the given steps-

- The conjunction 'that' should be used in place of a comma (,) and inverted commas (" ").
- 'Said to' is changed into 'told'.
- The present continuous tense (is playing) is changed into the past continuous tense (was playing).

Hence, the correct option is (A).

24. Vasanth told Praveen that he had eaten three apples.

While changing the narration of an assertive sentence, we need to follow the given steps-

- The conjunction 'that' should be used in place of a comma (,) and inverted commas (" ").
- 'Said to' is changed into 'told'.
- The present perfect tense (have eaten) is changed into the past perfect tense (had eaten).
- The first-person (I) is changed into the third-person (he) i.e. subject of the reporting verb. (Vasanth)

Hence, the correct option is (C).

25. Anitha said that she had been learning Bharatanatyam for the past six months.

While changing the narration of an assertive sentence, we need to follow the given steps-

- The conjunction 'that' should be used in place of a comma (,) and inverted commas (" ").
- 'Said' remains unchanged.
- The present perfect continuous tense (have been learning) is changed into the past perfect continuous tense (had been learning).
- The first-person (I) is changed into the third-person (she) i.e. subject of the reporting verb. (Anitha)

Hence, the correct option is (A).

26. Sunder said that he would go to his sister's house that day.

While changing the narration of an assertive sentence, we need to follow the given steps-

- The conjunction 'that' should be used in place of a comma (,) and inverted commas (" ").
- 'Said' remains unchanged.
- 'Will' is changed into 'would'.
- The first-person (I/my) is changed into the third-person (he/his) i.e. subject of the reporting verb. (Sunder)
- 'Today' is changed into 'that day'.

Hence, the correct option is (D).

27. Nisha told Sunil that she would not be going for the class.

While changing the narration of an assertive sentence, we need to follow the given steps-

- The conjunction 'that' should be used in place of a comma (,) and inverted commas (" ").
- 'Said to' is changed into 'told'.
- 'Will' is changed into 'would'.
- The first-person (I) is changed into the third-person (she) i.e. subject of the reporting verb. (Nisha)

Hence, the correct option is (C).

28. The stranger enquired where I lived.

While changing the narration of an interrogative sentence, we need to follow the given steps-

- A conjunction is not used in the sentence of wh-family words (what, where, who, whom, why, etc.).
- 'Question mark (?)' is changed to full stop (.).
- 'Said' will be changed into 'asked/ enquired'.
- 'Do + v1 (live)' is changed into 'v2' (lived) in indirect speech.
- 2nd person (you) is changed into (I).

Hence, the correct option is (A).

29. The judge commanded to call the first witness.

While changing the narration of an imperative sentence, we need to follow the given steps-

- 'Said' is changed into 'ordered/commanded/ requested/ advised'.
- The conjunction 'to' should be used in place of a comma (,) and inverted commas (" ").
- At last line up the remaining sentence.

Hence, the correct option is (D).

30. Siva said that he had read the novel Pride and Prejudice.

While changing the narration of an assertive sentence, we need to follow the given steps-

- The conjunction 'that' should be used in place of a comma (,) and inverted commas (" ").
- 'Said' remains unchanged.
- The present perfect tense (have read) is changed into the past perfect tense (had read).
- The first-person (I) is changed into the third-person (he) i.e. subject of the reporting verb. (Siva)

Hence, the correct option is (C).

Ques (1-9):Directions: Sentences are given with blanks to be filled in with an appropriate word(s). Four alternatives are suggested for each question. Choose the correct alternative out of the four.

Q.1 ________ pollution control measures are expensive, many industries hesitate to adopt them.

A. Although **B.** However
C. Because **D.** Despite

Q.2 There is something wonderful __ him.

A. of **B.** about **C.** for **D.** inside

Q.3 On my return from a long holiday, I had to ________ with a lot of work.

A. Catch on **B.** Catch up **C.** Make up **D.** Take up

Q.4 The deserted garden was infested ________ weeds.

A. With **B.** For **C.** Into **D.** On

Q.5 The song in the play cannot be deleted it is ________ to the story.

A. Intervened **B.** Innate
C. Exacting **D.** Integral

Q.6 700 men worked for 10 years to ________ the Borobudur temple in Java to its former glory.

A. Restore **B.** Give **C.** Create **D.** Revive

Q.7 Each school has its own set of rules ________ all good pupils should follow them.

A. But **B.** Or **C.** Else **D.** And

Q.8 It is time we ________ with determination.

A. Act **B.** Acted
C. Have acted **D.** Will act

Q.9 When the thief entered the house, the inmates ________ in the hall.

A. Were slept **B.** Were sleeping
C. Slept **D.** Had been sleeping

Q.10 Direction: Complete the given sentence using the appropriate pronoun from the following options:

This is the boy _____ scored the highest marks.

[Allahabad High Court Review Officer (RO), 2019]

A. it **B.** whose **C.** which **D.** who

Q.11 Direction: Fill in the blank with the most appropriate option as given:

Giving money to the poor is a/an _____ act of service to the poor.

[Allahabad High Court Review Officer (RO), 2019]

A. benevolent **B.** bemused
C. atrocious **D.** bad

Q.12 Direction: Among the following options, select the word that can best complete the given sentence:

When I met Ram yesterday, it was the first time I _____ him since my graduation.

[Allahabad High Court Review Officer (RO), 2019]

A. met **B.** had been meet
C. have meet **D.** have been seeing

Q.13 Direction: Fill in the blank by choosing the correct preposition from the following options:

Everything _____ this store is for sale.

[Allahabad High Court Review Officer (RO), 2019]

A. on **B.** in **C.** through **D.** over

Q.14 Direction: Fill in the blank with the appropriate option:

The teacher complained _____ him when she met his mother in the market.

[Allahabad High Court Review Officer (RO), 2019]

A. in **B.** against **C.** on **D.** by

Q.15 Direction: Fill in the blank using the options given below:

The activity that you are doing should _____ your interest.

[Allahabad High Court Review Officer (RO), 2019]

A. peak **B.** pique **C.** peek **D.** peke

Q.16 Direction: Fill in the blanks with the correct form of the word given in the brackets.

My guide _____ (tell) me If I wanted to meet these people, I would have to walk two miles.

[Allahabad High Court Review Officer (RO), 2019]

A. telling **B.** tell **C.** told **D.** has tell

Ques (17-29):Direction: Following sentence has a blank space and four words or group of words given after the sentence. Select the word or group of words you consider most appropriate for the blank space.

Q.17 There was a time when West Germany was a distinct _____.

[UPSC NDA, 2021]

A. policy **B.** polity
C. abstract **D.** hierarchy

Q.18 I was _____ with the film, I had expected it to be better.

[UPSC NDA, 2021]

A. disappointed **B.** disappointing
C. annoying **D.** prejudiced

Q.19 It was a _____ experience. Everybody was shocked.

[UPSC NDA, 2021]

A. terrified **B.** horrified
C. terrifying **D.** denouncing

Q.20 Elephants _____ when they perceive danger.

[UPSC NDA, 2021]

A. trumpet **B.** frolic **C.** whine **D.** sing

Q.21 The first film on Tagore was such a success that now they are going to make a _____.

[UPSC NDA, 2021]

A. serial **B.** sequence
C. sequel **D.** sequential

Q.22 The United Nations had ______ 2020 as the International Year of Plant Health.

[UPSC NDA, 2021]

A. ruled **B.** ordered **C.** foretold **D.** declared

Q.23 My brother is ____ punctual, but he is late today.

[UPSC NDA, 2021]

A. normatively **B.** primarily
C. normally **D.** basically

Q.24 The pleasant _____ of the rain as it fell on the dust made me feel nostalgic.

A. incense **B.** balm **C.** aroma **D.** perfume

Q.25 Moviemakers generally _____ historical facts to write their stories.

A. explain **B.** correct **C.** account **D.** adapt

Q.26 If only we ______ as we were told! This would never have happened.

A. had done **B.** would have done
C. did **D.** was done

Q.27 Peter wants to come ______ us this summer.

A. at **B.** with **C.** by **D.** in

Q.28 They weren't going to do that, _____ ?

A. Do they? **B.** Were they?
C. Are they? **D.** Weren't they?

Q.29 The thorns on the rose plant are for protection ______ predators.

A. by **B.** through **C.** between **D.** against

Q.30 A rattlesnake's fangs ______ neatly folded away when not in use but are swung forward for the strike.

A. is **B.** are **C.** thus **D.** but

// Smart Answer Sheet //

Correct — Indicates percentage of students who answered questions correctly.

Skipped — Indicates percentage of students who skipped questions.

Q.	Ans.	Correct	Skipped
1	C	89.82 %	10.12 %
2	B	81.02 %	12.73 %
3	B	88.32 %	10.95 %
4	A	76.39 %	18.61 %
5	D	81.61 %	14.45 %
6	A	79.89 %	17.73 %
7	D	76.29 %	22.93 %
8	B	80.4 %	10.77 %
9	B	88.1 %	10.22 %
10	D	83.26 %	15.89 %
11	A	84.18 %	14.75 %
12	A	85.99 %	11.19 %
13	B	81.61 %	16.76 %
14	B	84.74 %	10.97 %
15	A	78.35 %	17.81 %
16	C	77.25 %	18.5 %
17	B	83.58 %	11.7 %
18	A	86.01 %	12.4 %
19	C	82.64 %	13.75 %
20	A	78.8 %	13.48 %
21	C	78.05 %	20.17 %
22	D	78.65 %	16.63 %
23	C	89.87 %	10.02 %
24	C	79.73 %	14.38 %
25	D	85.99 %	12.05 %
26	A	84.48 %	12.07 %
27	B	89.15 %	10.48 %
28	B	78.13 %	21.32 %
29	D	88.14 %	10.74 %
30	B	86.01 %	11.51 %

Performance Analysis	
Avg. Score (%)	56.67%
Toppers Score (%)	70.0%
Your Score	

//Hints and Solutions//

1. The correct word will be `because'.

The sentence implies here the reason as to why many industries hesitate to adopt pollution control measures.

Complete sentence is "Because pollution control measures are expensive, many industries hesitate to adopt them."

Hence, the correct option is (C).

2. The presposition `About' is correct here.

Complete sentence is "There is something wonderful **about** him."

The most common meaning of about as a preposition is 'on the subject of' or 'connected with'. 'About' can be used as a preposition to mean 'on the subject of' or 'concerning', such as in:

- We talked about her new job.
- The lights were scattered about the room.

Hence, the correct option is (B).

3. The idiom that fits perfectly is 'catch up'.

Complete sentence is "On my return from a long holiday, I had to **catch up** with a lot of work."

Use of catch up:

- Catch up means to do tasks which one should have done earlier.
- Catch on means to be popular.
- Make up means to compensate.
- Take up means to pursuit.

Hence, the correct option is (B).

4. Complete sentence is "The deserted garden was infested **with** weeds."

Infested with - overspread, in large numbers, typically so as to cause damage or disease.

Use of preposition with: It is used to indicate being together or being involved.

- **Example**: I ordered a sandwich with a drink.

So usage of preposition `with' after infested is correct.

Hence, the correct option is (A).

5. The correct answer is "Integral".

Complete sentence is "The song in the play cannot be deleted it is **integral** to the story."

The meaning of integral is elementary, fundamental, anything which is not omittable, removable. The sentence implies here that song in that play is not removable as it is part of that story or it is fundamental to story.

Hence, the correct option is (D).

6. The correct answer is "Restore".

Complete sentence is "700 men worked for 10 years to **restore** the Borobudur temple in Java to its former glory."

Restore: renewal, revival, reestablishment

- **Example**: You have restored my faith in humanity.

The tone of the sentence is that the temple was bring back to its glory, and its synonym is 'restore'.

Hence, the correct option is (A).

7. The correct answer is "and".

Complete sentence is "Each school has its own set of rules **and** all good pupils should follow them."

The sentences on either side of the blank talks about rules and following them, thus 'but' and 'else' should not be filled, thus the conjunction that perfectly fits here is 'and'.

Use of and: The word and is a conjunction, and when a conjunction joins two independent clauses, you should use a comma with it. The proper place for the comma is before the conjunction.

- **Example**: On Monday we'll see the Eiffel Tower, and on Tuesday we'll visit the Louvre.

Hence, the correct option is (D).

8. The correct answer is "acted".

Complete sentence is "It is time we **acted** with determination."

Acted: to do something, to take action

- **Example**: She learned at an early age how to act properly in social situations.

The sentence expresses something that should have happened in the past, thus 'acted' fits it perfectly.

Hence, the correct option is (B).

9. The correct answer is "were sleeping".

Complete sentence is "When the thief entered the house, the inmates **were sleeping** in the hall."

The first part of the sentence is in the past tense. So the second must be in past continuous, thus the correct answer is 'were sleeping'.

Hence, the correct option is (B).

10. This is the boy who scored the highest marks.

The most suitable pronoun for the given blank is 'who'. A pronoun is a word that replaces a noun to avoid its repetition.

A relative pronoun is one which is used to refer to nouns mentioned previously, whether they are people, places, things, animals, or ideas" (i.e. Who, whom, that, which, etc.). Who should be used to refer to the subject of a sentence.

For example: Jack is the one who wants to go.

Hence, the correct option is (D).

11. Correct sentence: Giving money to the poor is a/an **benevolent** act of service to the poor.

Benevolent: kind and helpful, giving money or help to people or organizations that need it.

According to the given sentence, giving money to the poor is an act of charity. Therefore, we need a word whose meaning is close to kind/helpful.

So, according to the context of the sentence, 'benevolent' fits appropriately in the given blank.

Hence, the correct option is (A).

12. Correct sentence: When I met Ram yesterday, it was the first time I met him since my graduation.

The first part of the given sentence is in the Past Tense. Since the principal clause of the sentence is in the past tense, the following clause will also be in the past tense.

For example: When I went for the interview on Monday, I saw Kiya for the first time since my college.

So, 'met' is the appropriate word to be used.

Hence, the correct option is (A).

13. Everything **in** this store is for sale.

The most appropriate preposition for the given blank is 'in.'

A preposition is a word or group of words used before a noun, pronoun, or noun phrase to show direction, time, place, location, spatial relationships, or to introduce an object. To refer to a place, use the prepositions "in".

Here, in the given blank, the preposition 'in' is used to show the place where everything is for sale.

For example: They will meet in the lunchroom.

Hence, the correct option is (B).

14. Correct Sentence: The teacher complained **against** him when she met his mother in the market.

We use in to talk about where something is in relation to a larger area around it.

- Example: She's in the garden.

We use against to refer to negative, hostile or opposing reactions to situations, beliefs, people, events, etc.

- The noun 'complaint' is followed by the preposition against.
  - Example: He filed a complaint against his school.

"On" is used to indicate position, usually indicating that something is on top of something else.

- Example: My journal is on the desk.

When we use the passive voice, we can use a phrase with by to say who did the action.

- Example: The new street was opened by the Mayor.

Hence, the correct option is (B).

15. The activity that you are doing should **peak** your interest.

In this blank, we need a word whose meaning is close to 'to reach the highest point.'

- Peak: to reach the highest, strongest, or best point, value, or level of skill.
- Pique: to excite or cause interest.
- Peek: to look, especially for a short time or while trying to avoid being seen.
- Peke: a small dog with long, soft hair and a wide, flat nose.

Hence, the correct option is (A).

16. Correct sentence: My guide **told** me If I wanted to meet these people, I would have to walk two miles.

The second part of the given sentence is in the Past Tense.

When the second part of the sentence is in the Past Tense, then the first part of the sentence must be in the Past Tense.

- For example: John left and I arrived at the office.

The past tense of the verb tell is 'told.'

Hence, the correct option is (C).

17. There was a time when West Germany was a distinct **polity**.

In the given sentence, we need a word close to the meaning of 'an organized society' to fill in the blank.

The meanings of the given words:

- Polity: an organized society; a state as a political entity.
- Policy: a course or principle of action adopted or proposed by an organization or individual.
- Abstract: a summary of the contents of a book, article, or speech.
- Hierarchy: a system in which members of an organization or society are ranked according to relative status or authority.

From the meanings of the words, we can say that 'polity' is the most appropriate answer.

Hence, the correct option is (B).

18. I was **disappointed** with the film, I had expected it to be better.

In the given sentence, we need a word close to the meaning of 'displease' to fill in the blank. In this sentence, we need a Past Participle form of the verb.

The meanings of the given words:

- Disappointed: failed to fulfil the hopes or expectations of.
- Disappointing: failing to fulfil the hopes or expectations of.
- Annoying: making (someone) a little angry; irritate.
- Prejudiced: gave rise to prejudice in (someone), made biased.

From the meanings of the words, we can say that ''disappointed' is the most appropriate answer.

Hence, the correct option is (A).

19. It was a **terrifying** experience. Everybody was shocked.

In the given sentence, we need a word (adjective) close to the meaning of 'extreme fear' to fill in the blank.

The meanings of the given words:

- Terrifying (Adjective): causing extreme fear.
- Terrified (Verb): caused to feel extreme fear.
- Horrified: filled with horror; extremely shocked.
- Denouncing: publicly declaring to be wrong or evil.

From the meanings of the words, we can say that 'terrifying' is the most appropriate answer.

Hence, the correct option is (C).

20. Elephants **trumpet** when they perceive danger.

In the given sentence, we need a word close to the meaning of 'to produce a loud scream or call (for elephants)' to fill in the blank.

The meanings of the given words:

- Trumpet: (of a large animal, especially an elephant) to produce a loud call.
- Frolic: play or move about in a cheerful and lively way.
- Whine: give or make a long, high-pitched complaining cry or sound.
- Sing: make a high-pitched whistling or buzzing sound.

From the meanings of the words, we can say that 'trumpet' is the most appropriate answer.

Hence, the correct option is (A).

21. The first film on Tagore was such a success that now they are going to make a **sequel**.

In the given sentence, we need a word close to the meaning of 'continuation' to fill in the blank.

The meanings of the given words:

- Sequel: a published, broadcast, or recorded work that continues the story or develops the theme of an earlier one.
- Serial: a story or play appearing in regular instalments on television or radio or in a magazine.
- Sequence: a particular order in which related things follow each other, continuation.
- Sequential: forming or following in a logical order or sequence.

From the meanings of the words, we can say that 'sequel' is the most appropriate answer.

Hence, the correct option is (C).

22. The United Nations had **declared** 2020 as the International Year of Plant Health.

In the given sentence, we need a word close to the meaning of 'announced' to fill in the blank.

The meanings of the given words:

- Declared: said something in a solemn and emphatic manner, announced.
- Ruled: to have the power over a country, group of people, etc.
- Ordered: to use your position of authority to tell somebody to do something or to say that something must happen.
- Foretold: predicted (the future or a future event).

From the meanings of the words, we can say that 'declared' is the most appropriate answer.

Hence, the correct option is (D).

23. My brother is **normally** punctual, but he is late today.

In the given sentence, we need a word close to the meaning of 'usually' to fill in the blank.

The meanings of the given words:

- Normally: under normal or usual conditions; as a rule.
- Normatively: implying, creating, or prescribing a norm or standard.
- Primarily: for the most part; mainly.
- Basically: in the most essential respects; fundamentally.

From the meanings of the words, we can say that 'normally' is the most appropriate answer.

Hence, the correct option is (C).

24. The pleasant aroma of the rain as it fell on the dust made me feel nostalgic.

According to the given sentence, the pleasant smell of the rain made the speaker nostalgic.

The word 'aroma' means 'a smell, especially a pleasant one'. Example: The aroma of cologne surrounded him and his breath smelled like he had recently brushed his teeth.

So, according to the context of the sentence, 'aroma' fits appropriately in the given blank.

Hence, the correct option is (C).

25. Moviemakers generally adapt historical facts to write their stories.

According to the given sentence, moviemakers adapt historical facts to write stories.

The word 'adapt' means alter (a text) to make it suitable for filming, broadcasting, or the stage.

Example: He needed to adapt his strategies when dealing with her.

So, according to the context of the sentence, 'adapt' fits appropriately in the given blank.

Hence, the correct option is (D).

26. Correct Sentence: If only we had done as we were told! This would never have happened.

Conditional sentences are statements discussing known factors or hypothetical situations and their consequences.

One of the structures is mentioned below:

- This particular type is followed when we talk about something in the past which is purely imaginary.
- If + Subject + had + V_3+ object, Subject + Would have +V_3+ Object.

Example:

- If I had noticed you, I would have called you.

As per the rule and example have given above, 'had done' will be used in the blank part of the sentence.

Hence, the correct option is (A).

27. Correct sentence is: Peter wants to come with us this summer.

- The sentence talks about peter who wants to spend the summer.
- Here, peter intends to accompany them this summer. 'with' means accompanied by (another person or thing).
- So, 'with' is the correct word for the blank.

Hence, the correct option is (B).

28. The correct answer is 'were they?'.

- The given sentence is in the form of a question tag.
- Here, the verb is 'going' which has the helping verb 'weren't', so the tag must be 'were they?' because the helping verb is 'weren't' and it is a negative sentence.
- In question tags, if the sentence is positive then the tag is negative and vice versa.

Hence, the correct option is (B).

29. The correct answer is 'against'.

'against' is the correct solution because it means to be prepared for a difficulty or in case of. 'between' is wrong because it is used in the comparison between two things. 'by' is wrong as it means from where it is from. 'through' means to move in one side which is also wrong.

So, the correct solution is: The thorns on the rose plant are for protection against predators.

Hence, the correct option is (D).

30. The correct answer is 'are'.

Nouns such as pliers, trousers, pants, fangs, tongs, proceeds, etc. exist only in plural forms. They take plural verbs with them.

For eg: The proceeds were deposited in the bank.

So, we will use 'are' to fill in the blank to complete the sentence meaningfully.

Hence, the correct option is (B).

Q.1 Direction: Select the most appropriate meaning of the underlined idiom in the given sentence.

If the audit report shows anomalies, the finance manager will be brought to book.

[SSC CGL, 2020]

A. Held accountable **B.** Rewarded suitably
C. Supported fully **D.** Given a promotion

Q.2 Direction: Select the most appropriate meaning of the underlined idiom in the given sentence.

His comments cast a slur upon the integrity of his manager.

[SSC CGL, 2020]

A. Damaged **B.** Redeemed
C. Praised **D.** Improved

Q.3 Direction: Select the most appropriate for the phrase.

Hard-nosed attitude

A. Quality to forgive **B.** Protective
C. Aggressive **D.** Calm

Q.4 Direction: Select the option that means the same as the given idiom.

Alive and kicking

A. To be dead inside **B.** To excel
C. Lively and active **D.** To participate

Q.5 Direction: Select the most appropriate meaning of the underlined idiom in the given sentence.

Dowry is a burning question of the day.

A. A widely debated issue
B. A dying issue
C. A relevant problem
D. An irrelevant issue

Q.6 Direction: In the following question, out of the four alternatives, choose the alternative which best expresses the meaning of the Idiom/Phrase.

A peeping Tom

A. Tom is peeping from the door.
B. Tom is a cheat.
C. A person working for Police.
D. A person who secretly watches others, especially for sexual gratification.

Q.7 Direction: In the following question, out of the four alternatives, choose the alternative which best expresses the meaning of the Idiom/Phrase.

Achilles heel

A. Runaway
B. Soft feet
C. A small problem or weakness in a person or system that can result in failure
D. Walk slowly

Q.8 Direction: In the following question, out of the four alternatives, select the alternative which best expresses the meaning of the Idiom/Phrase.

Fit as a fiddle

A. To play a melodious tune
B. In a perfectly healthy condition
C. A severe and conclusive test
D. To be a perfect match

Q.9 Direction : In the following questions, four/five alternatives are given for the meaning of the given Idiom/Phrase. Choose the alternative which best express the meaning of the Idiom/Phrase.

To pick holes

A. To find some reason to quarrel
B. To destroy something
C. To cut some part of an item
D. To criticise someone

Q.10 Direction: Select the most appropriate meaning of the underlined idiom in the given sentence.

If I say "I am going to hit the books now".

A. Take a short break from studying
B. Throw my books away
C. To study
D. Worry about study

Q.11 Direction: In the given question, four alternatives are given for the meaning of the given Idiom/Phrase. Choose the alternative which best express the meaning of the Idiom/Phrase.

Off the hook

A. Everything prepared and kept ready for you.
B. Accept something without checking its veracity.
C. No longer in difficulty or trouble.
D. Put a person who is helping you into a difficult situation.

Ques (12-21):Direction: Given below idioms/phrases followed by four alternative meanings to each. Choose whichever is the most appropriate meaning and mark your answer.

Q.12 Overstep the mark

[UPSC NDA, 2021]

A. To tell people how successful you are
B. To step into someone else's areas of expertise
C. To upset someone by doing/saying more than you should
D. To do something in an excited way

Q.13 Palsy-walsy friends

[UPSC NDA, 2021]

A. Good friends
B. Friends who help each other in difficult suituations
C. Friends by choice, and not by chance

D. Unfriendly

Q.14 Open a Pandora's box

[UPSC NDA, 2021]

A. To do something that causes a lot of new problems that you did not expect
B. To do something out of compulsion
C. To do something beyond expectation
D. To do something out of the box, that causes awards and ceremonies for you

Q.15 Pull your socks up

[UPSC NDA, 2021]

A. To get well - dressed for the occasion
B. Improve your work or behaviour
C. To speak in an honest way without hesitation
D. To be in control of an organization, often secretly

Q.16 To get under somebody's skin

[UPSC NDA, 2021]

A. To deceive someone
B. To admire someone
C. To annoy someone
D. To support someone

Q.17 Turn topsy-turvy

[UPSC NDA, 2021]

A. To completely change something
B. To completely evaluate something
C. To enjoy yourself greatly
D. To exhaust yourself completely

Q.18 A clarion call

[UPSC NDA, 2021]

A. A trumpet call
B. An intimidating voice
C. A strong request
D. An urgent order

Q.19 Fire in the belly

[UPSC NDA, 2021]

A. Fear and hatred
B. Powerful ambition
C. Love and affection
D. Lethargy and indifference

Q.20 A hunky-dory situation

[UPSC NDA, 2021]

A. There are serious issues among people
B. There are no problems and people are happy
C. There is war and bloodshed all over
D. There is no work, only enjoyment

Q.21 Give somebody a leg up

[UPSC NDA, 2021]

A. To pull someone down
B. To deceive and betray someone
C. To help someone for their livelihood
D. To help someone to be successful

Q.22 Direction: Fill in the blank and complete the idiom:
They had successfully hidden the news of their venture from everyone. It was now time to let the _____ out of the bag.

[Allahabad High Court Review Officer (RO), 2019]

A. dog **B.** toy **C.** cat **D.** cards

Q.23 Direction: Select the most appropriate meaning of the underlined idiom in the given sentence.
I told you not to play the prank but you didn't listen, now <u>face the music.</u>

A. accept the consequences
B. put on earphones
C. listen to the songs
D. sing popular songs

Q.24 Direction: Select the most appropriate meaning of the underlined idiom in the given sentence.
This problem is <u>a hard nut to crack</u>, it will take longer than they imagined.

A. involves breaking nuts
B. is not interesting enough
C. is difficult to solve
D. needs a lot of work

Q.25 Direction: Choose the option which best expresses the meaning of the idiom/phrase given below.
"Let sleeping dogs lie"

A. To get someone drunk
B. A fair competition where no side has an advantage
C. To make a dog sleep
D. To avoid restarting a conflict

Q.26 Direction: Choose the option which best expresses the meaning of the idiom/phrase given below.
"To pick holes"

A. To lose courage
B. To be afraid to die
C. To find the weak points in something
D. To articulate clearly

Q.27 Direction: Choose the option which best expresses the meaning of the idiom/phrase given below.
"Flog a dead horse"

A. To bear the brunt of
B. To criticise someone
C. To be evil tempered
D. To waste your effort by trying to do something that is no longer possible

Q.28 Direction: In the following question, out of the four alternatives, select the alternative which best expresses the meaning of the idiom/phrase.
In a flutter

A. In a hard-pressed situation
B. In a confused and excited state
C. In an embarrassing situation
D. None of these

Q.29 Direction: In the following question, out of the four alternatives, choose the alternative which best expresses the meaning of the Idiom/Phrase.

All in all

A. Every person

B. Particular thing same in all

C. Call all at once

D. Most important

Q.30 Direction: In the following question, out of the four alternatives, choose the alternative which best expresses the meaning of the Idiom/Phrase.

At close quarters

A. close examinations

B. live near to each other

C. live far to each other

D. in love

// Smart Answer Sheet //

Correct Indicates percentage of students who answered questions correctly.

Skipped Indicates percentage of students who skipped questions.

Q.	Ans.	Correct	Skipped
1	A	86.61 %	13.28 %
2	A	76.45 %	13.04 %
3	C	84.84 %	13.51 %
4	C	81.0 %	16.37 %
5	A	86.34 %	10.42 %
6	D	83.2 %	12.7 %
7	C	79.96 %	20.01 %
8	B	89.49 %	10.36 %
9	D	78.44 %	15.2 %
10	C	83.91 %	15.91 %
11	C	82.73 %	13.44 %
12	C	77.38 %	13.87 %
13	A	88.11 %	10.87 %
14	A	87.76 %	11.79 %
15	B	80.98 %	10.81 %
16	C	82.39 %	15.01 %
17	A	87.28 %	11.28 %
18	C	76.99 %	16.17 %
19	B	78.55 %	16.58 %
20	B	82.45 %	17.23 %
21	D	80.84 %	14.1 %
22	C	80.01 %	12.01 %
23	A	88.19 %	10.44 %
24	C	80.98 %	18.03 %
25	D	81.61 %	12.37 %
26	C	89.17 %	10.56 %
27	D	79.51 %	18.85 %
28	B	83.81 %	12.81 %
29	D	85.92 %	14.02 %
30	A	76.45 %	23.4 %

Performance Analysis	
Avg. Score (%)	50.0%
Toppers Score (%)	63.33%
Your Score	

//Hints and Solutions//

1. The correct answer is 'held accountable.'

Brought to book- to reprimand or require (someone) to give an explanation of his conduct.

Example:

If policemen have lied, then they must be brought to book.

Hence, the correct option is (A).

2. The correct answer is- 'damaged'.

Cast a slur upon- to bring discredit or disgrace, damage

Example:

Manny's elopement with her boyfriend cast a slur upon her family.

Hence, the correct option is (A).

3. Hard nose attitude: being tough, stubborn, or uncompromising

For example, That guy seems so hard-nosed that I'm afraid to say hi to him.

Thus, 'aggressive' is the most suitable meaning.

Hence, the correct option is (C).

4.

- The idiom, 'Alive and kicking' means continue to live or exist and be full of energy.
- For example, She hadn't met her younger sister after her marriage and was delighted to see her alive and kicking at a social event last weekend.

Hence, the correct option is (C).

5. Burning question: an important question that requires an answer or a question whose answer is of great interest to everyone.

For example: Real estate taxes are always a burning question for the town leaders.

Hence, the correct option is (A).

6. The idiom A peeping Tom refers to a person who secretly watches others.

Example: Reynolds contended that the Chinese man was a peeping tom whom he caught spying on his wife one last night March while she was toweling herself after a shower.
Hence, the correct option is (D).

7. The correct answer is 'a small problem or weakness in a person or system that can result in failure'.

Someone's Achilles heel is the weakest point in their character or nature, where it is easiest for other people to attack or criticize them.

Example- His Achilles heel is his quick temper.
Hence, the correct option is (C).

8. The phrase "fit as a fiddle" is a simile that means being in good health; something that's in sound condition.

e.g. - He is fit as a fiddle for this job.

Hence, the correct option is (B).

9. To pick holes means To make an effort to find flaws or negative aspects in something through excessive analysis or criticism.
Hence, the correct option is (D).

10. Hit the Books: To study and to begin to study in a serious and determined way.

Example: "Danny was in danger of failing, so before his last math test he left the show early to go home and hit the books."

Hence, the correct option is (C).

11. Off the hook - No longer in difficulty or trouble.

e.g. At first, Sam was suspected of stealing money from the safe, but he was let off the hook after security camera footage showed it was someone else.

Hence, the correct option is (C).

12. Overstep the mark: To upset someone by doing/saying more than you should

The meaning of the 'Overstep the mark' is to go beyond what is proper or allowed by something.

Example: She warned us not to overstep the mark.

Hence, the correct option is (C).

13. The meaning of the 'Palsy-walsy friends' is good friends, pals, or buddies.

Example: I'm surprised you haven't met Ravi's new palsy-walsy friends from school yet.

Hence, the correct option is (A).

14. The meaning of 'Open a Pandora's box' is to do something that creates a lot of new problems that you did not expect.

Example: Sadly, his reforms opened up a Pandora's box of domestic problems.

Hence, the correct option is (A).

15. The meaning of 'Pull your socks up' is to make an effort to improve your work or behaviour because it is not good enough.

Example: He's going to have to pull his socks up if he wants to stay in the team.

Hence, the correct option is (B).

16. The meaning of 'To get under somebody's skin' is to annoy someone.

Example: Jack really gets under my skin - he never buys anyone a drink.

Hence, the correct option is (C).

17. The meaning of 'Turn topsy-turvy' is to be confused, or lacking organization, change completely, upside down.

Example: Things are so topsy-turvy at work these days.

Hence, the correct option is (A).

18. The meaning of 'A clarion call' is a strongly expressed demand or request for action.

Example: He issued a clarion call to young people to join the Party.

Hence, the correct option is (C).

19. The meaning of 'Fire in the belly' is a powerful sense of ambition or determination.

Example: He lacks the fire in his belly necessary to seek the presidency.

Hence, the correct option is (B).

20. "A hunky-dory situation" means there are no problems and people are happy.

Example: You can't lose your temper one minute and then expect everything to be hunky-dory again the next.

Hence, the correct option is (B).

21. The meaning of 'Give somebody a leg up' is to help someone to improve their situation, especially at work.

Example: These skills will give you a leg up in the job market.

Hence, the correct option is (D).

22. Correct sentence: They had successfully hidden the news of their venture from everyone. It was now time to let the cat out of the bag.

The most suitable word to complete the idiom is 'cat.'

Let the cat out of bag means- "to allow something that is hidden to be revealed". For **Example:** I have let the cat out of the bag, there is no point pretending that this job is working out for me.

Hence, the correct option is (C).

23. To face the music means to accept the consequences.

For eg- He would later have to face the music for his improper decisions.

Hence, the correct option is (A).

24. A Hard nut to crack - a problem that is very difficult to solve or a person who is very difficult to understand.

For Example: The test problem was a hard nut to crack.

Hence, the correct option is (C).

25. The meaning of the given idiom 'Let sleeping dogs lie' is 'to avoid restarting a conflict or ignore a problem because trying to deal with it could cause an even more difficult situation'.

Examples:

- I thought about bringing up my concerns but decided instead to let sleeping dogs lie.
- If he hasn't said anything about the incident, just let sleeping dogs lie.

Hence, the correct option is (D).

26. The meaning of the given idiom 'to pick holes' is 'To make an effort to find flaws or negative aspects in something through excessive analysis or criticism.'

Examples:

- Critics picked holes in his performance, but fans seemed to love it.
- It's easy for him to pick holes in my explanation.

Hence, the correct option is (C).

27. The meaning of the given idiom 'Flog a dead horse' is 'To continue to focus on some issue or topic that is no longer of any use or relevance.'

Examples:

- We've all moved on from that problem, so there's no use flogging a dead horse.
- We are flogging a dead horse in still trying to promote the scheme.

Hence, the correct option is (D).

28. "In a flutter" means in a confused and excited state.

Hence, the correct option is (B).

29. All in all means the most important thing or person.

Example: As she is only girl in a big family, so she is all in all in her home.

Hence, the correct option is (D).

30. At close quarters means close examinations.

For example: Real friends never leave us alone in close quarters.

Hence, the correct option is (A).

Ques (1-30):Direction: In the following question, out of the four alternatives, choose the one which can be substituted for the given sentence.

Q.1 A nature reserve for birds or animals
A. Sanctuary **B.** Retreat
C. Oasis **D.** Asylum

Q.2 A particular form of a language which is peculiar to a specific region.
A. Dialect **B.** Slang **C.** Jargon **D.** Lingo

Q.3 A young person tending to commit a crime, particularly minor crime.
A. Criminal **B.** Derelict
C. Delinquent **D.** Convict

Q.4 A factual written account of important or historical events in the order of their occurrence.
[IDBI Bank Assistant Manager, 2019]
A. Journal **B.** Chronicle
C. Manuscript **D.** Register

Q.5 One who works for the good of others
[SSC Selection Post Phase IX, 2019]
A. Antagonist **B.** Atheist
C. Altruist **D.** Agnostic

Q.6 That which cannot be avoided
A. Inevitable **B.** Irreparable
C. Incomparable **D.** Indisputable

Q.7 One who able to use the right and left hands equally well
A. Sinister **B.** Ambidextrous
C. Ambivalent **D.** Amateur

Q.8 "Government by rich, wealthy people"
A. Oligarchy **B.** Aristocracy
C. Pantisocracy **D.** Plutocracy

Q.9 An independent person or body officially appointed to settle a dispute.
A. Arbiter **B.** Mediator
C. Agent provocateur **D.** Arbitrator

Q.10 A country that constitutionally ensures equal rights for all citizens
A. An autocracy **B.** A theocracy
C. A democracy **D.** A dictatorship

Q.11 A person who knows and speaks several languages fluently
A. A polymath **B.** A translator
C. A polyglot **D.** An interpreter

Q.12 Someone who runs away from the law.
A. A delinquent **B.** A juvenile
C. An exile **D.** A fugitive

Q.13 A person who was arrested for marrying multiple times
A. Bigamy **B.** Polygamy
C. Endogamy **D.** Monogamy

Q.14 A doctor who takes care of newborn infants
A. A urologist **B.** An epidemiologist
C. A neonatologist **D.** A pediatrician

Q.15 One who does not drink alcohol
A. Vegetarian **B.** Faithful
C. Virtuous **D.** Teetotaler

Q.16 One who makes an official examination of accounts
A. Controller **B.** Supervisor
C. Auditor **D.** Officer

Q.17 One who feeds on human flesh
A. Cannibal **B.** Omnivorous
C. Vegan **D.** Carnivorous

Q.18 A life history written by somebody else
A. Autobiography **B.** Museology
C. Biography **D.** Bibliography

Q.19 A man who is womanish in his habits
[HTET TGT Mathematics, 2019], [HTET TGT Science, 2019]
A. Feminist **B.** Philologist
C. Effeminate **D.** Philanderer

Q.20 An ill-tempered scolding woman
A. Vindicate **B.** Virago
C. Vigour **D.** Vicarious

Q.21 A person who creates disorder in a state
A. Rebel **B.** Fifth Columnist
C. Militant **D.** Anarchist

Q.22 A place where bees are kept
A. A pantry **B.** A nursery
C. An apiary **D.** An aquarium

Q.23 One who makes maps or charts
A. Cartoonist **B.** Cartographer
C. Choreographer **D.** Choirmaster

Q.24 A form of utopian social organization (in which all are equal in social position and responsibility).
A. Monarchy **B.** Pantisocracy
C. Plutocracy **D.** Autocracy

Q.25 A style in which a writer makes a display of his knowledge.
A. Pedantic **B.** Verbose

C. Pompous **D.** Ornate

Q.26 The dates when days and nights are of equal length.
[SSC Sub Inspector (CPO), 2020]

A. Equinox **B.** Solstice **C.** Eclipse **D.** Stellar

Q.27 Something which is considered to be very important.

A. Cardinal **B.** Scanty
C. Meager **D.** Supplementary

Q.28 A place where dogs are kept

A. Stable **B.** Kennel
C. Sty/ pigsty **D.** Cattery

Q.29 The life history of a person written by himself.

A. Essay **B.** Biography
C. Travelogue **D.** Autobiography

Q.30 A person of evil reputation

A. Renowned **B.** Famous
C. Notorious **D.** Icon

// Smart Answer Sheet //

Correct Indicates percentage of students who answered questions correctly.

Skipped Indicates percentage of students who skipped questions.

Q.	Ans.	Correct	Skipped
1	A	85.55 %	13.07 %
2	A	83.78 %	14.61 %
3	C	84.01 %	10.63 %
4	B	85.13 %	12.22 %
5	C	87.48 %	12.16 %
6	A	87.21 %	12.57 %
7	B	82.98 %	13.62 %
8	D	79.05 %	14.61 %
9	D	85.73 %	12.28 %
10	C	79.77 %	12.53 %
11	C	84.88 %	13.98 %
12	D	88.27 %	10.97 %
13	B	86.72 %	10.55 %
14	C	76.22 %	23.39 %
15	D	82.14 %	16.92 %
16	C	82.48 %	15.66 %
17	A	84.58 %	11.41 %
18	C	79.46 %	12.94 %
19	C	82.87 %	12.24 %
20	B	81.23 %	18.07 %
21	D	81.52 %	14.9 %
22	C	80.04 %	11.28 %
23	B	77.62 %	19.14 %
24	B	89.16 %	10.13 %
25	A	86.11 %	11.69 %
26	A	80.14 %	13.08 %
27	A	77.26 %	10.0 %
28	B	77.32 %	15.01 %
29	D	79.47 %	11.28 %
30	C	86.72 %	12.83 %

Performance Analysis	
Avg. Score (%)	40.0%
Toppers Score (%)	53.33%
Your Score	

//Hints and Solutions//

1. 'Sanctuary' is a nature reserve for birds or animals.

Example: The animal sanctuary is a no-kill shelter that provides abandoned animals with safe homes.

Hence, the correct option is (A).

2. 'Dialect' is a particular form of a language which is peculiar to a specific region or social group.

Example: The play was hard to understand when the characters spoke in dialect.

Hence, the correct option is (A).

3. 'Delinquent' means (typically of a young person) tending to commit a crime, particularly minor crime.

Example: His delinquent behavior could lead to more serious problems.

Hence, the correct option is (C).

4. 'Chronicle' is a factual written account of important or historical events in the order of their occurrence.

Example: He has produced a chronicle of his life during the war years.

Hence, the correct option is (B).

5. Let us look at the meaning of the given words:

Altruist: A person who is concerned about the welfare of others

Antagonist: A person who is hostile to someone

Atheist: A person who does not believe in God

Agnostic: a person who believes that nothing is known or can be known of the existence or nature of God

Thus, option (C) is the most appropriate alternative to the given group of words.

Hence, the correct option is (C).

6. That which cannot be avoided- Inevitable

- Inevitable: certain to happen, unavoidable.
- Irreparable: impossible to rectify or repair.
- Incomparable: without an equal in quality or extent, matchless.
- Indisputable: unable to be challenged or denied.

Hence, the correct option is (A).

7. Ambidextrous: able to use the right and left hands equally well.

Sinister: One who able to use the left hand well.

Ambivalent: having mixed feelings or contradictory ideas about something or someone.

Amateur: a person who is contemptibly inept at a particular activity.

Hence, the correct option is (B).

8. Plutocracy: government by rich, wealthy people.

Oligarchy: a small group of people having control of a country or organization.

Aristocracy: a form of government in which power is held by the nobility.

Pantisocracy: a form of utopian social organization in which all are equal in social position and responsibility.

Hence, the correct option is (D).

9. Arbitrator: an independent person or body officially appointed to settle a dispute.

Arbiter: a person who settles a dispute or has ultimate authority in a matter.

Mediator: a person who attempts to make people involved in a conflict come to an agreement; a go-between.

Agent provocateur: a person employed to induce others to break the law so that they can be convicted.

Hence, the correct option is (D).

10. A country that constitutionally ensures equal rights for all citizens is called a **democracy**.

- Democracy: a government or country that is elected by the people, or a government in which the supreme power is vested in the people and exercised by them directly or indirectly through a system.
- Autocracy: a government or country that is ruled by one person who has complete power.
- Theocracy: a government or country in which priests rule in the name of God or a god.
- Dictatorship: a government or country in which total power is held by a dictator or a small group.

Hence, the correct option is (C).

11. Polyglot: a person who knows/writes/speaks more than one language.

- Polymath: a person of wide knowledge or learning.
- Translator: a person who changes something that has been written or spoken from one language to another.
- Interpreter: a person whose job is to translate what somebody is saying immediately into another language.

From the meanings, it is clear that Polyglot is a word that can replace the phrase.

Hence, the correct option is (C).

12. Fugitive: a person who is running away or escaping from the police or do any crime.

- Delinquent: a person who behaves badly and often breaks the law.
- Juvenile: young people who are not yet adults.
- Exile: a person who is forced to live outside his/her own country (especially for political reasons).

From the meanings, it is clear that Fugitive is a word that can replace the phrase.

Hence, the correct option is (D).

13. He was arrested for marrying multiple times, and so he was charged with **polygamy**.

- Polygamy: the custom of having more than one wife at the same time.
- Bigamy: the state of being married to two people at the same time.
- Endogamy: the custom of marrying only within the limits of a local community, clan, or tribe.
- Monogamy: the fact or custom of being married to only one person at a particular time.

Hence, the correct option is (B).

14. A doctor who takes care of newborn infants is called a **neonatologist**.

- A urologist is a physician who specializes in diseases of the urinary tract.
- An epidemiologist is a doctor who specializes in the occurrence, distribution, and control of epidemic diseases.
- A pediatrician is a doctor who deals with the diseases of children.

Hence, the correct option is (C).

15. Teetotaler: a person who does not drink alcohol

Therefore, the word 'teetotaler' is the meaning of the given group of words.

- Vegetarian: a person who does not eat meat or fish
- Faithful: true-hearted or devoted
- Virtuous: spiritual or relating to religion

Hence, the correct option is (D).

16. Auditor- someone whose job is to carry out an official examination of the accounts of a business and to produce a report.

- Controller- a person who controls something, or someone who is responsible for what a particular organization does.
- Supervisor- a person whose job is to supervise someone or something.
- Officer- a person who has a position of authority in an organization.

Hence, the correct option is (C).

17. Cannibal- a person who eats human flesh, especially for magical or religious purposes.

- Omnivorous- (of an animal or person) feeding on a variety of food of both plant and animal origin.
- Vegan- a person who does not eat any food derived from animals and who typically does not use other animal products.
- Carnivorous- (of an animal) feeding on other animals.

Hence, the correct option is (A).

18. Biography: an account of someone's life written by someone else.

- Autobiography: an account of a person's life written by that person.
- Museology: the science or practice of organizing, arranging, and managing museums.
- Bibliography: a list of the books referred to in a scholarly work, typically printed as an appendix.

Hence, the correct option is (C).

19. A man who is womanish in his habits is called effeminate.

- A person who supports feminism is called a feminist.
- A person who studies language in oral and written historical sources is called a philologist.
- A man who readily or frequently enters into casual sexual relationships with women is called a philanderer.

Hence, the correct option is (C).

20. 'Virago' is a 'noun' which means 'a bad-tempered woman who is aggressive and tries to tell people what to do'.

- 'Vindicate' is a 'verb' which means 'to prove that somebody is not guilty when they have been accused of doing something wrong or illegal'.
- 'Vigour' is a 'noun' which means 'strength or energy'.
- 'Vicarious' is an adjective which means 'felt or experienced by watching or reading about somebody else doing something, rather than by doing it yourself'.

Hence, the correct option is (B).

21. 'Anarchist' is a person who rebels against any authority, established order, or ruling power. Therefore, "A person who creates disorder in a state" is Anarchist.

- 'Rebel' is a person who rises in opposition or armed resistance against an established government or leader.
- 'Fifth Columnist' is a group of secret sympathizers or supporters of an enemy that engages in espionage or sabotage within defense lines or national borders.
- 'Militant' is one who is intensely or excessively devoted to a cause.

Hence, the correct option is (D).

22. 'An apiary' is a place where bees are kept; a collection of beehives.

- 'A pantry' is a small room or cupboard in which food, crockery, and cutlery are kept.
- 'A nursery' is a place where young plants and trees are grown for sale or for planting elsewhere.
- 'An aquarium' is a transparent tank of water in which live fish and other water creatures and plants are kept.

Hence, the correct option is (C).

23. A cartographer is a person who draws or produces maps.

- A cartoonist is a visual artist who specializes in drawing cartoons (individual images) or comics (sequential images).
- A choreographer is a person who composes the sequence of steps and moves for a performance of dance.
- A Choirmaster is the conductor of a choir.

Hence, the correct option is (B).

24. Pantisocracy: A form of utopian social organization (in which all are equal in social position and responsibility).

- Monarchy means a system of government characterized by a king queen as ahead of the government.
- Plutocracy means rule by the wealthy or power provided by wealth.
- Autocracy means one person possesses unlimited power.

Hence, the correct option is (B).

25. A style in which a writer makes a display of his knowledge- Pedantic

In other words, Pedantic is an insulting word used to describe someone who annoys others by correcting small errors, caring too much about minor details, or emphasizing their own expertise especially in some narrow or boring subject matter.

- Verbose: Using more words that are needed.
- Pompous: Self-important
- Ornate: Elaborately adorned

Hence, the correct option is (A).

26. Equinox- the time or date (twice each year) at which the sun crosses the celestial equator, when day and night are of approximately equal length (about September 22 and March 20)

- Solstice- the time or date (twice each year) at which the sun reaches its maximum or minimum declination, marked by the longest and shortest days (about June 21 and December 22)
- Eclipse- an obscuring of the light from one celestial body by the passage of another between it and the observer or between it and its source of illumination
- Stellar- relating to a star or stars

Hence, the correct option is (A).

27. Something which is considered to be very important is 'Cardinal'.

- Scanty: smaller in size or amount than is considered necessary or is hoped for.
- Meager: (of amounts or numbers) very small or not enough.
- Supplementary: added to something else in order to improve it or complete it.

Hence, the correct option is (A).

28. Kennel - a small, usually wooden, shelter for a dog to sleep in outside. Plural: Kennels

- Stable: A place where horses are kept
- Sty/ pigsty: A place where pigs are kept
- Cattery: A place where cats are kept

Hence, the correct option is (B).

29. Autobiography- an account of a person's life written by that person

- Essay- a short piece of writing on a particular subject
- Biography- an account of someone's life written by someone else
- Travelogue- a movie, book, or illustrated lecture about the places visited and experiences encountered by a traveler

Hence, the correct option is (D).

30. Notorious- famous or well known, typically for some bad quality or deed

- Renowned- known or talked about by many people; famous
- Icon- a person or thing regarded as a representative symbol or as worthy of veneration

Hence, the correct option is (C).

Q.1 Direction: Given below are four sentences in jumbled order. Pick the option that gives their correct order.

A. Therefore, I bought a good house in a respectable neighborhood.

B. This made me eager to welcome the first guest at home and show my hospitality.

C. I intended to be a model citizen in the neighborhood.

D. I decided it was time for me to settle down.

[SSC CGL, 2020]

A. DBCA **B.** CBDA **C.** DACB **D.** CADB

Ques (2-3):Direction: In the following question, sentences of a paragraph have been jumbled and labeled as A, B, C and D. You are required to rearrange the jumbled sentences of the paragraph and mark your response accordingly by selecting the correct option.

Q.2 A. The forest and trees filter the air and absorb harmful gases.

B. The environment gives us countless benefits that we can't repay our entire life.

C. Plants purify water, reduce the chances of a flood, maintain a natural balance, and many more.

D. As they are connected with the forest, trees, animals, water, and air.

A. CDAB **B.** BDCA **C.** ABCD **D.** BDAC

Q.3 A: Hence, they are the most useful members of any society.

B: No one can deny that farmers form the backbone of any nation

C: They grow food for the whole country.

D: Yet they don't get the profit and recognition which they deserve.

A. ADCB **B.** CADB **C.** DCBA **D.** BCAD

Q.4 Direction: In the following question, sentences of a paragraph have been jumbled and labeled as A, B, C and D. You are required to rearrange the jumbled sentences of the paragraph and mark your response accordingly by selecting the correct option.

A. But this drive expresses itself in many different ways.

B. Nietzsche sees the will to power as neither good nor bad.

C. According to him, it is a basic drive found in everyone.

D. The philosopher and the scientist direct their will to power into a will to truth.

A. DCAB **B.** ADCB **C.** CDAB **D.** BCAD

Ques (5-7):Direction: Sentences of a paragraph are given below in jumbled order. Arrange the sentences in the right order to form a meaningful and coherent Sentence.

Q.5 Let us all be

P) until we realise

Q) we are all the same

R) unique together

A. QPR **B.** PRQ **C.** PQR **D.** RPQ

Q.6 The author has chosen

P) on this story

Q) responses

R) not to show

A. PQR **B.** QPR **C.** RQP **D.** PRQ

Q.7 Seeking help

P) always easy

Q) is not

R) for everyone

A. PQR **B.** QPR **C.** RPQ **D.** QRP

Q.8 Direction: Arrange these parts so as to form a complete meaningful sentence/paragraph and then choose the correct combination.

Environmental protection

P: and management is.

Q: deservedly attracting a lot.

R: of attention these days.

A. PQR **B.** PRQ **C.** QPR **D.** RPQ

Q.9 Direction: Arrange these parts so as to form a complete meaningful sentence/paragraph and then choose the correct combination.

Propensity to addiction

P: predisposition of the individual.

Q: in other words, is not a.

R: but the result of the social contest.

A. PRQ **B.** PQR **C.** RPQ **D.** QPR

Q.10 Direction: Arrange these parts so as to form a complete meaningful sentence/paragraph and then choose the correct combination.

Don't leave something good

P-because once you realize

Q-to find better

R-you had the best, the best has found better

A. RPQ **B.** QPR **C.** PQR **D.** QRP

Q.11 Direction: Arrange these parts so as to form a complete meaningful sentence/paragraph and then choose the correct combination.

Life appears to me

P- too short to be spent

Q- or registering wrongs

R- in nursing animosity

A. PQR **B.** PRQ **C.** RPQ **D.** QPR

Q.12 Direction: In the following question, sentences of a paragraph have been jumbled and labeled as A, B, C and D. You are required to rearrange the jumbled sentences of the paragraph and mark your response accordingly by selecting the correct option.

A. One of the best-known examples of North Indian sculpture.
B. And hints at the richness and grandeur of the ancient Mauryan Empire.
C. Is the Lion Capital of Ashoka, Sarnath.
D. It is the source for the national emblem of India.

A. ABDC **B.** ACDB **C.** ADCB **D.** ABCD

Q.13 Direction: Select the option that gives their correct order.

A. Then he started on his eighteen kilometer expedition back to his village.
B. Mohan first equipped himself with a long, sturdy stick.
C. At several points, he lost the road and had to swim his way ahead.
D. It was a journey he would never forget where he had to use his stick constantly to locate the road.

A. BADC **B.** ACBD **C.** CDBA **D.** DCAB

Ques (14-16):Direction: Given below are four jumbled sentences. Select the option that gives their correct order.

Q.14 A: Tansen was their only child.
B: It is said that he was a naughty child.
C: Often, he ran away to play in the forest and soon learnt to imitate perfectly the calls of birds and animals.
D: A singer called Mukandan Misra and his wife lived in Behat near Gwalior.

A. DABC **B.** ABDC **C.** BCAD **D.** CBAD

Q.15 A: It is not one long bone from the upper arm to our wrist.
B: It is different bones joined together at the elbow.
C: Bones cannot be bent.
D: So, how do we bend our elbow?

A. ABDC **B.** CDAB **C.** DABC **D.** BCDA

Q.16 A. Then she has breakfast at 6:30.
B. Every morning she wakes up at six o'clock.
C. After breakfast, she helps her aunt with the house chores for an hour.
D. First she collects the eggs and feeds the chicken.

A. ACDB **B.** BDAC **C.** CDAB **D.** DACB

Ques (17-19):Direction: In these question, some parts of the sentence have been jumbled up. You are required to rearrange these parts which are labeled P, Q, R and S to produce the correct sentence. Choose the proper sequence.

Q.17 A. His mother was dead.
B. They had not sent him the sad information.
C. Probably they knew his deep love for her.
D. When Gandhi returned to India his son Hiralal was four.

A. CDAB **B.** DABC **C.** DBAC **D.** DCAB

Q.18 A. It results from a carefully revised plan.
B. Men work together for a cause or purpose.
C. Team work does not just happen.
D. It must be clearly known to them.

A. BCAD **B.** CBDA **C.** BCDA **D.** CABD

Q.19 A. I will give you a copy of it.
B. The book was published in New York.
C. It is a very interesting book.
D. It deals with mankind's political future.

A. DCBA **B.** CBDA **C.** BDCA **D.** DBCA

Ques (20-23):Direction: Rearrange the following given sentences to make a meaningful paragraph and then choose the correct order from the options given below.

Q.20 P. was capable of improving
Q. and in terms of number, but it was not to be
R. The strong Indian contingent for the Athens Olympics
S. both in terms of the quality of medal

A. SQRP **B.** RPSQ **C.** SPRQ **D.** RQSP

Q.21 P. as long-term growth prospects remain strong
Q. In the recent months the growth of the mobile companies
R. but it seems to be blip
S. has slowed down

A. QPRS **B.** RSQP **C.** QSRP **D.** RPQS

Q.22 P. that even five hours later there was no proper estimate
Q. The delay meant that not only did the monster tsunami wave
R. of the true magnitude of the grave tragedy
S. strike without warning but

A. RSPQ **B.** QPSR **C.** RPSQ **D.** QSPR

Q.23 P. into a fully integrated biotechnology enterprise
Q. focused on healthcare
R. In the years, that followed, Bicon evolved
S. from an industrial enzymes company

A. RSPQ **B.** QSRP **C.** RPSQ **D.** QPRS

Ques (24-26):Direction: Arrange these parts so as to form a complete meaningful sentence/paragraph and then choose the correct combination.

Q.24 A: by her indulgent parents
B: the child was so spoiled
C: when she did not receive all of their attention
D: that she pouted and became sullen
Which of the sequences present the most logical sentence?

A. CBAD **B.** BCAD **C.** BADC **D.** BDAC

Q.25 A : an image of a person in meditative pose
B : surrounded by animal, wild and tame
C : we have in the relics of Mohenjodaro
D : with eyes closed and indrawn
Which of the sequences present the most logical sentence?

A. CADB **B.** ABCD **C.** CBAD **D.** CABD

Q.26 A : for the future

B : and poses the major challenge

C : commercial energy consumption

D : shows an increasing trend

Which of the sequences present the most logical sentence?

A. CDBA **B.** CDBA **C.** ADCB **D.** ABCD

Ques (27-28):Direction: Given below are four sentences in jumbled order. Pick the option that gives their correct order.

Q.27 A. Mummy struggled to pull them apart and finally succeeded.

B. She tried to get them to make up but they did not listen.

C. It was a fierce fight, of course.

D. The two children scratched and hit each other.

A. ACBD **B.** DBAC **C.** CBDA **D.** CDAB

Q.28 A. But he seems to have become weary when it came to the ears.

B. The result is that we spend all our hours hankering after something unattainable, namely silence.

C. God constructed the human body with a lot of forethought and solicitude.

D. He left them as the most vulnerable part of a human being.

A. CDBA **B.** CADB **C.** DABC **D.** BCDA

Ques (29-30):Direction: Given below are four sentences in jumbled order. Pick the option that gives their correct order.

Q.29 A. Soon, Mahima's castle was ready.

B. As for Sudhir's castle, even the walls weren't ready yet.

C. It was beautiful with big and small domes and arches.

D. Sudhir and Mahima settled down on the sand and each began to make a separate castle.

A. CBDA **B.** ABDC **C.** DBCA **D.** DACB

Q.30 A. He had lost his leg in an accident five years back.

B. With that accident, his dream of becoming the next Carl Lewis had been shattered forever.

C. In place of his left leg was a wooden stump.

D. Vikas sat up and removed the bed sheet that was covering his leg.

A. DCAB **B.** ACDB **C.** BCAD **D.** CDAB

// Smart Answer Sheet //

Correct — Indicates percentage of students who answered questions correctly.

Skipped — Indicates percentage of students who skipped questions.

Q.	Ans.	Correct	Skipped
1	C	78.18 %	21.22 %
2	D	79.89 %	17.39 %
3	D	89.16 %	10.35 %
4	D	78.99 %	10.72 %
5	D	85.95 %	11.82 %
6	C	82.8 %	12.16 %
7	B	81.81 %	10.89 %
8	A	78.15 %	20.26 %
9	D	83.07 %	12.01 %
10	B	81.8 %	15.4 %
11	B	87.06 %	12.23 %
12	B	76.26 %	13.9 %
13	A	79.09 %	18.05 %
14	A	80.8 %	10.97 %
15	B	81.86 %	10.05 %
16	B	83.88 %	14.62 %
17	B	77.71 %	11.68 %
18	D	89.53 %	10.27 %
19	C	81.64 %	10.07 %
20	B	80.91 %	18.06 %
21	C	80.63 %	18.26 %
22	D	83.53 %	15.2 %
23	A	84.84 %	12.91 %
24	C	86.39 %	12.93 %
25	A	84.8 %	10.0 %
26	B	86.09 %	12.06 %
27	D	77.54 %	10.76 %
28	B	87.94 %	10.46 %
29	D	81.59 %	10.64 %
30	A	79.13 %	17.12 %

Performance Analysis	
Avg. Score (%)	60.0%
Toppers Score (%)	70.0%
Your Score	

//Hints and Solutions//

1. The correct order is 'DACB'.

In the given question Part D will be the first statement because the first statement of a sentence jumbled question is usually an independent general statement, a noun, a universal fact, starting of an incident, or it starts with 'most' or 'once'.

Part D will be the first sentence because it is the starting of an incident.

Part D describes that the writer has decided to settle down.

And Part A explains what the writer did to settle down. Therefore, the next sentence will be Part A.

Part A is connected with Part C because it tells what the writer intends to do after buying a house. Hence, Part C will be the next sentence.

And Lastly, Part B will come because it shows how the writer decides to implement what he said in Part C.

Hence, the correct option is (C).

2. The given paragraph is related to the importance of the environment. So, sentence 'B' will be the first sentence after rearrangement as it establishes the subject matter. The word 'they' in the sentence 'D' is used for 'countless benefits' mentioned in sentence 'B' so it will be followed by sentence 'D'. Sentence 'A' follows 'D' as it talks about the 'benefits of trees and forests' and is in the continuation of 'D'. Sentence 'C' is the logical successor of 'A' as it further explains the 'benefits of plants'.

Thus, the correct arrangement is BDAC.

Hence, the correct option is (D).

3. B is the sentence that introduces the topic- farmers. So, it will be the first sentence after rearrangement.

C follows B as it gives the reason for what is mentioned in B.

A follows C as it starts with 'hence' showing that it is indeed right to say that farmers are the most useful members of society.

D follows A as it connects with it by yet. 'Yet' signifies 'still'. Farmers are the most useful members of society, still, they don't get much profit or recognition.

Thus, the correct arrangement is: BADC

Hence, the correct option is (D).

4. When ordering the sentences, it is easier to find the first few and then eliminate the options. The first sentence is always independent and introduces a topic. Here, only sentence B is independent and introduces the topic of 'Nietsche and will to power'. So, B must be the first sentence. This order is only shown by option (D).

Thus, the correct sequence is: BCAD.

Hence, the correct option is (D).

5. The starting statement starts with 'let us', the continuing statement will be talking about the uniqueness of all i.e. R. P follows R as it describes up to when we all can be unique. Q will be the concluding statement as it talks about the realisation that we all are same. The correct option is RPQ as only that arrangement would make a coherent paragraph.

The correct formation would be, 'let us all be unique together until we realise, we all are the same'.

Hence, the correct option is (D).

6. Since the statement talks about the choice of an author, the continuing statement would be his choice of not showing responses on something. So, R follows Q and P will be the concluding statement as he chooses not to respond on his writings. Thus, the correct option is RQP as only that arrangement would make a coherent paragraph.

The correct formation would be, 'The author has chosen not to show responses on this story'.

Hence, the correct option is (C).

7. As the starting statement talks about the seeking help, the next statement would be carrying a verb, so, Q follows. P follows Q as it describes that taking help is not that easy. R will be the concluding statement as it states that it is not easy for everyone. Thus, the correct option is QPR as only that arrangement would make a coherent paragraph.

The correct formation would be, 'Seeking help is not always easy for everyone'.

Hence, the correct option is (B).

8. it is clear from the first sentence that it must followed by P because of the conjunction 'and'. Q must be followed by R, as they form a logical pair and sentence can't end with 'a lot' so, sentence ends with R.

Hence, the correct option is (A).

9. A given sentence can follow P or Q, not R as R contains 'but', therefore we must use a contradictory sentence before that. Q followed by P as it can't be followed by R because 'not' must follow a sentence i.e. P, and lastly, P followed by R. The correct sequence is "Propensity to addiction, in other words, is not a predisposition of the individual but the result of the social contest."

Hence, the correct option is (D).

10. Q makes a logical pair with the given sentence "Don't leave something good". Now P and R follow Q Because it provides the reason for why we should not leave good in search of better. Thus QPR is the correct logical sequence.

Hence, the correct option is (B).

11. It makes sense that only P follows the given statement as all others are inappropriate. R followed by Q due to the presence of 'or' conjunction.

Hence, the correct option is (B).

12. The sentence 'A' starts the paragraph by pointing towards the North Indian Sculpture. Therefore, A is the first part.

The sentence 'C' completes the sentence 'A'. as the best-known example is the Sarnath. Therefore, C is the second part.

The pronoun 'It' mentioned in the sentence 'D' refers back to the noun 'Sarnath' mentioned in the sentence 'C'. Therefore, D follows C.

The sentence 'B' is concluding the paragraph. Therefore, it is the last part.

Thus, the correct sequence is: ACDB.

Hence, the correct option is (B).

13. The correct order is BADC.

Mohan first equipped himself with a long, sturdy stick. Then he started on his eighteen kilometer expedition back to his village. It was a journey he would never forget where he had to use his stick constantly to locate the road. At several points, he lost the road and had to swim his way ahead.

- The first sentence would be 'B', as it's clearly mentioned the very first thing Mohan did.
- The second sentence is 'A', as it states the reason why Mohan took that sturdy stick.
- The third sentence will be 'D' which tells what this eighteen-kilometer expedition is.
- The last sentence is obviously 'C' that we are left with.

Hence, the correct option is (A).

14. From the given sentence,

Sentence D comes first as it is independent of any other sentence and opens the story.

Sentence A follows D as it has the pronoun 'their' that refers to persons mentioned in D.

Sentence B follows A as it has the pronoun 'he' that refers to Tansen, who is introduced in A.

Sentence C follows B as it further describes why Tansen was considered a naughty boy as mentioned in B.

Thus, the sequence becomes:

D: A singer called Mukandan Misra and his wife lived in Behat near Gwalior.

A: Tansen was their only child.

B: It is said that he was a naughty child.

C: Often, he ran away to play in the forest and soon learnt to imitate perfectly the calls of birds and animals.

Hence, the correct option is (A).

15. The correct order is CDAB.

From the given sentence,

Sentence C comes first as it is independent of any other sentence and introduces the matter of concern, i.e., bones.

Sentence D follows C as it asks a question that opposes the idea given in C.

Sentence A follows D as it states that the elbow can be bent because it is not one single bone.

Sentence B follows A as it further describes that the elbow is different bones joined together at the elbow.

Therefore, after applying the correct order, it'll become:

Bones cannot be bent. So, how do we bend our elbow? It is not one long bone from the upper arm to our wrist. It is different bones joined together at the elbow.

Hence, the correct option is (B).

16. The given question is an example of Sentence Jumble.

The first sentence of a sentence jumbled question is usually an independent general statement, a noun, a universal fact, statement regarding the starting of an incident or it starts with 'most' or 'once'.

From the given sentences it is evident that the passage presents a chronological order of the subject's daily morning routine.

Sentence B should start the passage as it points out when the subject wakes up in the morning.

Sentence D should come in the second position. It talks about the first actions performed by the subject after she wakes up.

Sentence A which points out the subject's breakfast time (the time mentioned is after the wake up time) should come in the third position.

Sentence C which points out what the subject does after breakfast rounds up the passage by coming in the fourth position.

Thus, the sequence becomes - Every morning she wakes up at six o'clock. First she collects the eggs and feeds the chicken. Then she has breakfast at 6:30. After breakfast, she helps her aunt with the house chores for an hour.

Hence, the correct option is (B).

17. The correct logical order is DABC.

D comes first as all other sentences follow the event mentioned in sentence D. A follows D joint by the pronoun 'his' mentioned in A and referring to Hiralal in D. B and C make a logical pair where C follows B because it describes the reason for not telling Gandhi about the death of his son's mother.

Hence, the correct option is (B).

18. The correct logical order is CABD.

The passage tells about teamwork and the opening sentence will be C introducing the topic. A follows C adding further information that team is not accidental but results from a carefully revised plan in which men work together as mentioned in B. D follows B joint by the pronoun 'it' mentioned in D referring to 'cause or purpose' in B.

Hence, the correct option is (D).

19. The correct logical order is BDCA.

The passage tells about book and the opening sentence will be B introducing the topic with 'the book'. D follows B adding further about the content of the book. D is followed by C which tells the speaker's opinion about the book which he/she proposes to lend a copy to the listener as mentioned in A.

Hence, the correct option is (C).

20. The correct order is RPSQ.

Sentence R is introducing sentence, now see sentence S, in this sentence we talked about two terms of strong Indian contingents out of which one term is given in the sentence but second is given in other sentence. In sentence Q another term is given thus it follows sentence S and sentence S follows sentence R.

Hence, the correct option is (B).

21. The correct order is QSRP.

Sentence Q is introducing sentence here and sentence S defines the growth of mobile companies in recent months has slow down, thus sentence S follows sentence Q. which is given in option C only.

Hence, the correct option is (C).

22. The correct order is QSPR.

Sentence Q is first sentence which start the paragraph with a subject. In the last of sentence Q given that 'the monster tsunami waves' now waves does 'strike' and this is given in sentence S, so sentence Q is followed by sentence S which is given only in option D.

Hence, the correct option is (D).

23. The correct order is RSPQ.

Look at sentence R, this is the only sentence which can start the paragraph, now it is given in sentence R 'Bicon evolved' , now sentence S can proceed this paragraph further and followed by sentence P. option A gives this sequence where sentence R followed by S and sentence S followed by P.

Hence, the correct option is (A).

24. B contains the subject 'the child' and is thus the first part. A will follow B because it is a passive sentence and the verb will be followed by the doer. D makes complete sense after A.

Complete sentence is: " The child was so spoiled by her indulgent parents that she pouted and became sullen when she did not receive all of their attention".

Hence, the correct option is (C).

25. C will be the first part since it contains the subject, B cannot preceed A as in (C) because B describes what is in A, so B will follow A and D.

Hence, the correct option is (A).

26. C is the opening sentence, since it introduces the subject, D describes what is said in C and thus will follow C. A will follow B, because the preposition 'for' will follow 'poses major challenge' and combines D and B, thus B follows.

Hence, the correct option is (B).

27. The correct order is - CDAB.

Sentence C introduces us to the subject 'fight'. It is the introductory sentence and will be put in the first place.

Sentence D tells us about the two children and their spat. It will be put in second place.

Sentence A tells us about the mother's successful intervention to end their quarrel. It will be put in third place.

The last sentence is B as it mentions the mother's attempt at the reconciliation between her children.

Hence, the correct option is (D).

28. The correct order is - CADB.

Sentence C introduces us to the subject 'God and the way he made the human body'. It is the introductory sentence and will be put in the first place.

Sentence A tells us about God's condition while making ears. It will be put in second place.

Sentence D tells us about the human ear as the most vulnerable part of the body. It will be put in third place.

The last sentence is B as it mentions the human's pursuit of silence.

Hence, the correct option is (B).

29. The correct order is 'DACB'.

Statement D introduces us to the vague subjects 'Sudhir and Mahima'. It is the introductory sentence and will be put in the first place.

Statement A tells us about the completion of Mahima's castle. It will be put in second place.

Statement C tells us about the specifications of the castle of Mahima. It will be put in third place.

Statement B as it mentions the progress of the castle of Sudhir. It will be put in fourth place.

Hence, the correct option is (D).

30. The correct order is "DCAB".

The sentence 'D' is independent of any other sentence as it is giving general information about "Vikas". So, 'D' is the first part.

The pronoun "his" mentioned in the sentence 'C' refers back to the noun 'Vikas' mentioned in the sentence 'D'. So, 'C' follows 'D'.

The 'leg' mentioned in the sentence 'A' refers back to the 'leg' mentioned in the sentence 'C'. So, 'A' follows 'C'.

The sentence 'B' is the concluding sentence. So, 'B' is the last sentence.

Hence, the correct option is (A).

Ques (1-5):Direction: Read the passage given below and answer the question that follow by selecting the most appropriate option.

When I was a boy in Dehra, there was a mango grove just opposite the bungalow. It belonged to someone called Seth Govind Ram (may his soul rest in peace), and, during the mango season, it was fiercely guarded by a giant of a man called Phambiri. All my efforts to get into the grove were repulsed, and on one occasion I received a mild lathi-blow on my backside.

'I just wanted to climb the tree' I pleaded.

'Come back when the mango season is over' said Phambiri with a vicious smile copied from a filmi villain.

And then I discovered that he was an ex-wrestler, that he had been a champion in his youth, and had even thrown the great King Kong, a famous wrestler from about forty years ago. (I did not know at the time that King Kong, in his bad years, was constantly being thrown out of the ring.) So, whenever I passed the grove and saw Phambiri, I would remark on his great strength, his superb condition (going to fat, really), his muscles like cricket balls, and his bull-like neck and shoulders.

Gradually he warmed to me, and began to tell me of his exploits. I acclaimed them. Then he showed me feats of strength, like picking up rocks and hurling them across the road. I applauded. Before long, he had invited me into the mango grove, and by the end of the week I could have all the mangoes I wanted. The guardian of the grove actually pressed them upon me.

Q.1 The man who guarded the mango grove was:

A. Looked like a giant **B.** Very persuasive
C. Armed with a sling **D.** Very gentle

Q.2 The mango grove was situated:

A. On the outskirts of Dehra
B. Beyond Mussourie
C. Near Seth Govind Ram's fields
D. Just opposite the bungalow inhabited by the narrator

Q.3 The guard's attitude to the boy changed because the boy:

A. Was terrified
B. Turned obedient
C. Started behaving like a filmy villain
D. Made him feel nice about himself

Q.4 The boy failed to get into the mango grove because:

A. He was too fat to do so.
B. He did not know how to climb the wall.
C. He was timid.
D. He was scared of the monstrous guard.

Q.5 The word 'exploits' used in the passage means:

A. Acts of meanness **B.** Acts of trickery
C. Acts of exploitation **D.** Acts of heroism

Ques (6-10):Direction: Read the passage given below and answer the questions that follow by selecting the most appropriate options:

One of the unhealthiest emotions is anger. It destroys our ability to think clearly, properly and in totality. Anger also has adverse impact on health. If you ask a selection of people what triggers their anger, you would get a wide range of answers. However, whatever the cause, even a single word spoken in anger can leave a lasting impression on a person's heart and has the ability to ruin the sweetness of any relationship.

A sage once said, "How can there be peace on earth if the hearts of men are like volcanoes ?" We can live in harmony with others only when we overcome anger and make room for peace. So how can we set about creating that sense of peace within ourselves ? It starts with the realisation that we do have the choice to think and feel the way we want to . If we look at what it is that makes us angry, we might discover there is nothing that has the power to make us feel this way. We can only allow something to trigger our anger — the anger is a way in which we respond to an event or person. But because we are so used to reacting on impulse, we forget to choose how we want to feel, and end up reacting inappropriately, leaving ourselves with angry feelings.

Meditation helps us create personal space within ourselves so that we have the chance to look, weigh the situation, and respond accordingly. remaining in a state of self-control. When we are angry, we have no self-control. At that moment, we are in a state of internal chaos, and anger can be a very destructive force.

Stability that comes from practice of meditation can create a firm foundation, a kind of positive stubbornness. Others can say whatever they want, and it may also be true, but we don't lose our peace or happiness on account of that. This is to respect what is eternal within each of us.

We give ourselves the opportunity to maintain our own peace of mind, because let's face it, no one's going to turn up at our door with a box full of peace and say, "Here, I think you could do with some of this today!" There is a method which could be described as sublimation, or the changing of form. With daily practice and application of spiritual principles in our practical life, experience of inner peace can come naturally.

Q.6 How can we get peace of mind?

[CTET Paper-II (Science & Mathematics), 2015], [CTET Paper-II (Social Science), 2015]

A. Through prolonged medication
B. By accepting life as it comes
C. By enjoying good health
D. By overcoming anger

Q.7 To overcome anger, meditation helps us by ______.

[CTET Paper-II (Science & Mathematics), 2015], [CTET Paper-II (Social Science), 2015]

A. removing the trigger
B. giving us the choice to think
C. remaining in a state of self-control
D. offering us a wide range of answers

Q.8 Why should we not get angry with a friend?
[CTET Paper-II (Science & Mathematics), 2015], [CTET Paper-II (Social Science), 2015]

A. It may give us a heart attack
B. It affects over health
C. It ruins our relationship
D. It damages our intellectual ability

Q.9 The antonym for the word, 'triggers' is:
[CTET Paper-II (Science & Mathematics), 2015], [CTET Paper-II (Social Science), 2015]

A. Excites **B.** Prolongs **C.** Deviates **D.** Controls

Q.10 The synonym for the word, 'adverse' is:
[CTET Paper-II (Science & Mathematics), 2015]

A. Angry **B.** Successful
C. Unfavourable **D.** Similar

Ques (11-15):Direction: Read the passage given below and answer the questions that follow by selecting the correct most appropriate options.

Each drop represents a little bit of creation and of life itself. When the monsoon brings to northern India the first rains of summer, the parched earth opens its pores and quenches its thirst with a hiss of ecstasy. After baking in the sun for the last few months, the land looks cracked, dusty and tired. Now, almost overnight, new grass springs up, there is renewal everywhere, and the damp earth releases a fragrance sweeter than any devised by man.

Water brings joy to earth, grass, leaf bud, blossom, insect, bird, animal and the pounding heart of man. Small children run out of their homes to romp naked in the rain. Buffaloes, which have spent the summer listlessly around lakes gone dry, now plunge into heaven of muddy water. Soon the lakes and rivers will overflow with the monsoon's generosity, Trekking in the Himalayan foothills, I recently walked for kilometres without encountering habitation. I was just scolding myself for not having brought along a water- bottle when I came across a patch of green on a rock face. I parted a curtain of tender maidenhair fern and discovered a tiny spring issuing from the rock-nectar for the thirsty traveller.

I stayed there for hours, watching the water descend, drop by drop, into a tiny casement in the rocks. Each drop reflected creation. That same spring, I later discovered, joined other springs to form a. swift, tumbling. stream, which went cascading down the hill into other streams until, in the plains, it became part of a river. And that river flowed into another mightier river that kilometres later emptied into the ocean. Be like water, taught Laotzu, philosopher 'and founder of Taoism. Soft and limpid, it finds its way through, over or under any obstacle. It does not quarrel; it simply moves on.

Q.11 Children respond to the first rains ofsummer by:
[CTET Paper - I, 2021]

A. Giving shouts of joy
B. Floating paper boats in the water
C. Running and playing in the rain
D. Singing songs

Q.12 The tiny spring issuing from the rockis hidden by:
[CTET Paper - I, 2021]

A. Thick moss **B.** Maidenhair fern
C. Bushes and creepers **D.** Tall grass

Q.13 To become part of a river, a tiny drophas to:
[CTET Paper - I, 2021]

A. Have a lot of strength
B. Depend on external forces
C. Suffer a lot
D. Merge its identity

Q.14 Which of the following words is mostsimilar in meaning to the word'pounding' as used in second para of thepassage?

A. Shaking **B.** Benumbing
C. Palpitating **D.** Sinking

Q.15 Which one of the following words ismost opposite in meaning to the word'descend' (para 3) as used in thepassage?
[CTET Paper - I, 2021]

A. Flow **B.** Ascend **C.** Hover **D.** Zoom

Ques (16-20):Direction: Read the passage given below and answer the question that follow by selecting the most appropriate option.

One day in 1924, five men who were camping in the Cascade Mountains of Washington saw a group of huge apelike creatures coming out of the woods. They hurried back to their cabin and locked themselves inside. While they were in, the creatures attacked them by throwing rocks against the walls of the cabin. After several hours, these strange hairy giants went back into the woods. After this incident the men returned to the town and told the people of their adventure. However, only a few people accepted their story. These were the people who remembered hearing tales about footprints of an animal that walked like a human being. The five men, however, were not the first people to have seen these creatures called Bigfoot. Long before their experience, local Native Americans were certain that a race of apelike animals had been living in the neighboring mountain for centuries. They called these creatures Sasquatch. In 1958, workmen, who were building a road through the jungles of Northern California often found huge footprints in the earth around their camp. Then in 1967, Roger Patterson, a man who was interested in finding Bigfoot went into the northern California jungles with a friend. While riding, they were suddenly thrown off from their horses. Patterson saw a tall apelike animal standing not far away. He managed to shoot seven rolls of film of the hairy creature before the animal disappeared in the hushes. When Patterson's film was shown to the public, not many people believed his story. In another incident, Richard Brown, a music teacher and also an experience hunter spotted a similar creature. He saw the animal clearly through the telescopic lens of his rifle. He said the creature looked more like a human than an animal. Later many other people also found deep footprints in the same area. In spite of regular reports of sightings and footprints, most experts still do not believe that Bigfoot really exists.

Q.16 What did the five campers do when they saw a group of apelike creatures?

A. They ran into the woods and hid there for several hours.
B. They quickly ran back into their cabin and locked the cabin door.
C. They threw rocks against the walls of their cabin to frighten the creatures away.
D. They attacked the creatures by throwing rocks at them.

Q.17 Did the town people believe the story of the five men about their meeting with Bigfoot?

A. No, not everyone believed their story.
B. Only those who had heard the same tale the second time believed them
C. Some said the five men were making up their own story.
D. All the people believed what they said..

Q.18 Who were the first people to have seen these apelike creatures before the five campers?

A. The workers who built the road in the jungles of Northern California.
B. Roger Patterson and his friend.
C. The local Native Americans.
D. Richard Brown, a music teacher and a hunter.

Q.19 The word 'neighbouring' would best be replaced with:

A. Far-off **B.** Nearby
C. Remote **D.** Far-away

Q.20 Who gave the name 'Sasquatch' to the apelike creatures?

A. The five campers
B. Roger Patterson
C. The local Native Americans
D. Richard Brown

Ques (21-25):Direction: Read the passage given below and answer the question that follow by selecting the most appropriate option.

Even though globalization is one of the most discussed topics in the contemporary world. It is not altogether a well-defined concept. A multitude of global interactions is put under the broad heading of globalization, varying from the expansion of cultural and scientific influences across borders to the enlargement of economic and business relations throughout the world. A wholesale rejection of globalization would not only go against global business, but it would also cut out movements of ideas, understanding, and knowledge that can help all the people of the world, including the most disadvantaged members of the world population. A comprehensive rejection of globalization can thus be powerfully counterproductive. There is a strong need to separate out the different questions that appear merged together in the rhetoric of the antiglobalization protests. The globalization of knowledge deserves a particularly high profile recognition, despite all the good things that can be rightly said about the importance of "Local knowledge".

Globalization is often seen, both in journalistic discussions and in remarkably many academic writings, as a process of westernization. Indeed, some who take an upbeat view of the phenomenon even see it as a contribution of Western civilization to the world.

Q.21 According to the passage, globalization is perceived often by media and academia as:

A. Supporting local knowledge system
B. Detrimental to local knowledge system
C. A process of Westernisation
D. A process of facilitating global business

Q.22 The attempt of a author in the passage is:

A. Unconditioned advocacy of globalization
B. Unconditioned rejection of globalization
C. Unconditioned rejection of local know ledge systems
D. Unbiased evaluation of globalization

Q.23 According to the passage, which one of the following is not a well-defined concept?

A. Multiculturalism **B.** Identity
C. Globalization **D.** Local knowledge

Q.24 As per the passage a wholesale reduction of globalization would result in affecting:

(a) Global businesses
(b) Movement of Ideas
(c) Local knowledge systems

Choose the correct answer from the options given below:

A. (a) and (b) only **B.** (a) and (c) only
C. (c) and (b) only **D.** (a), (b) and (c)

Q.25 According to the passage, which one of the following is counterproductive?

A. Comprehensive support to globalization
B. Wholesale rejection of globalization
C. Comprehensive rejection of anti-globalization protests
D. Recognition of local knowledge systems

Ques (26-30):Direction: Read the passage and answer the questions that follow.

Hideki Matsuyama was born in 1992. His father introduced him to golf when Matsuyama was only four years old. Matsuyama was very talented, and he won many golf championships. He was not a professional golf player until 2013. In March 2011, an earthquake and tsunami destroyed a big part of Japan, Matsuyama's home. In the same year, Matsuyama had his first chance to play in the Master's Tournament. He did not want to take part, but in the end, he decided that he would play. He wanted to make Japanese people happy again. In April 2021, he made Japanese people even happier when he won the Masters for the first time. He became the first Japanese man and the first Asian man in history to win. He won only by one shot over Will Zalatoris from the US.

Q.26 What is the Opposite word of Destroyed?

A. Demolish **B.** Conserved
C. Ruin **D.** Blast

Q.27 What changed the mind of Matsuyama to play golf for Masters?

A. To make his family happy again
B. To make Japanese people happy again
C. To fill proud for himself
D. To make his father happy again

Q.28 From whom, did Matsuyama win in Masters?

A. Will Zalatoris **B.** Jimmy Adams
C. Sam Adams **D.** Tiger Woods

Q.29 In which year, did Matsuyama win the Masters?

A. 1992 **B.** 2021 **C.** 2013 **D.** 2011

Q.30 Who introduced golf to Matsuyama?

A. Mother **B.** Brother **C.** Uncle **D.** Father

// Smart Answer Sheet //

Correct Indicates percentage of students who answered questions correctly.

Skipped Indicates percentage of students who skipped questions.

Q.	Ans.	Correct	Skipped
1	A	88.29 %	11.62 %
2	C	76.08 %	21.8 %
3	D	87.58 %	10.11 %
4	D	77.43 %	22.53 %
5	D	88.73 %	10.14 %
6	D	80.74 %	13.65 %
7	C	82.37 %	10.88 %
8	C	86.83 %	10.84 %
9	D	32.15 %	67.26 %
10	C	87.14 %	10.43 %
11	C	76.06 %	17.03 %
12	B	85.06 %	12.34 %
13	D	88.8 %	10.83 %
14	C	88.61 %	10.71 %
15	B	83.17 %	13.74 %
16	B	78.74 %	17.8 %
17	A	77.56 %	13.55 %
18	C	81.52 %	14.92 %
19	B	87.24 %	11.18 %
20	C	82.26 %	17.2 %
21	C	77.26 %	20.73 %
22	D	79.49 %	10.58 %
23	C	76.83 %	12.15 %
24	A	81.61 %	17.75 %
25	B	88.47 %	11.16 %
26	B	81.58 %	12.47 %
27	B	82.17 %	15.15 %
28	A	80.76 %	14.2 %
29	B	79.26 %	18.35 %
30	D	85.71 %	10.89 %

Performance Analysis	
Avg. Score (%)	40.0%
Toppers Score (%)	60.0%
Your Score	

//Hints and Solutions//

1. The man who guarded the mango grove was looked like a giant.

According to the passage, "When I was a boy in Dehra, there was a mango grove just opposite the bungalow. It belonged to someone called Seth Govind Ram (may his soul rest in peace), and, during the mango season, it was fiercely guarded by a giant of a man called Phambiri."

Hence, the correct option is (A).

2. The mango grove was situated near Seth Govind Ram's fields.

According to the passage, "When I was a boy in Dehra, there was a mango grove just opposite the bungalow. It belonged to someone called Seth Govind Ram (may his soul rest in peace), and, during the mango season, it was fiercely guarded by a giant of a man called Phambiri. All my efforts to get into the grove were repulsed, and on one occasion I received a mild lathi-blow on my backside."

Hence, the correct option is (C).

3. The guard's attitude to the boy changed because the boy made him feel nice about himself.

According to the passage, "Gradually he warmed to me, and began to tell me of his exploits. I acclaimed them. Then he showed me feats of strength, like picking up rocks and hurling them across the road. I applauded. Before long, he had invited me into the mango grove, and by the end of the week I could have all the mangoes I wanted. The guardian of the grove actually pressed them upon me."

Hence, the correct option is (D).

4. The boy failed to get into the mango grove because he was scared of the monstrous guard.

According to the passage, "When I was a boy in Dehra, there was a mango grove just opposite the bungalow. It belonged to someone called Seth Govind Ram (may his soul rest in peace), and, during the mango season, it was fiercely guarded by a giant of a man called Phambiri. All my efforts to get into the grove were repulsed, and on one occasion I received a mild lathi-blow on my backside."

Hence, the correct option is (D).

5. The word 'exploits' used in the passage means acts of heroism.

Exploit means a notable or heroic accomplishment.

Hence, the correct option is (D).

6. The following is mentioned in the passage:

"We can live in harmony with others only when we overcome anger and make room for peace."

Therefore, a person can get peace of mind when he/she overcomes anger.

Hence, the correct option is (D).

7. To overcome anger, meditation helps us by **remaining in a state of self-control.**

The following is mentioned in the passage:

- "Meditation helps us create personal space within ourselves so that we have the chance to look, weigh the situation, and respond accordingly remaining in a state of self-control."
- Meditation helps us to overcome anger because it teaches a person to remain in a state of self-control.

Hence, the correct option is (C).

8. The following is mentioned in the passage:

"However, whatever the cause, even a single word spoken in anger can leave a lasting impression on a person's heart and has the ability to ruin the sweetness of any relationship."

So, we should not get angry with a friend which may be painful for others and ruin the relationship.

Hence, the correct option is (C).

9. The meaning of the word 'triggers' is 'to activate or provoke or to give rise to'.

The meaning of the given words:

Controls: to remain calm or be in charge of or to manage

Excites: to provoke

Prolongs: to make longer

Deviates: to contrast with

Hence, the correct option is (D).

10. The meaning of the word 'adverse' is 'harmful or unfavourable'.

The meaning of the given words:

Unfavourable: expressing a lack of approval or unfriendly

Angry: full of anger

Successful: one who has achieved desired aim

Similar: close to or alike

Hence, the correct option is (C).

11. Children respond to the first rains of summer by running and playing in the rain.

According to the passage, 'Small children run out of their homes to romp naked in the rain.'

Romp means to play in a rough, excited, and noisy way. It can be concluded that the children played excitedly in the rain.

Hence, the correct option is (C).

12. According to the passage, 'I parted a curtain of tender maidenhair fern and discovered a tiny spring issuing from the rock-nectar for the thirsty traveller.'

Upon the perusal of the above statement, it can be concluded that the tiny spring issuing from the rock is hidden by maidenhair fern.

Hence, the correct option is (B).

13. According to the passage, 'I stayed there for hours, watching the water descend, drop by drop, into a tiny casement in the rocks.'

From the lines, it is evident that every drop of rain has its own identity which it represents and to become a part of the river it has to merge its identity.

Hence, the correct option is (D).

14. The meaning of given words:

- Pounding means the sound, feeling, or action of something beating repeatedly.
- Palpitating means (of the heart) beating rapidly and strongly.
- Benumbing means to make numb, especially by cold.
- Sinking means to go below the surface of water or another liquid.
- Shaking means to move backwards and forwards or up and down in quick, short movements, or to make something or someone do this.

Thus, palpitating and pounding are similar in meaning.

Hence, the correct option is (C).

15. The meaning of given words:

- Descend means move or fall downwards.
- Ascend means go up or climb.
- Hover means remain in one place in the air.
- Zoom means move or travel very quickly.
- Flow means the action or fact of moving along in a steady, continuous stream.

Thus, ascend and descend are opposite in meaning.

Hence, the correct option is (B).

16. Five men who were camping in the Cascade Mountains of Washington saw a group of huge apelike creatures coming out of the woods. They hurried back to their cabin and locked themselves inside.

Hence, the correct option is (B).

17. After the incident when five men saw the big foots they returned to the town and told the people of their adventure. However, only a few people accepted their story.

Hence, the correct option is (A).

18. The local native Americans were the first people to have seen these apelike creatures before the five campers.

Then in 1967, Roger Patterson, a man who was interested in finding Bigfoot went into the northern California jungles with a friend. While riding, they were suddenly thrown off from their horses. Patterson saw a tall apelike animal standing not far away. Therefore the first people to have seen these apelike creatures before the five campers was Roger Patterson and his friend.

Hence, the correct option is (C).

19. Neighbouring means: a person or place which is adjacent with the given person of place. Therefore nearby will be correct option which can replace the word 'neighbouring'

Hence, the correct option is (B).

20. The local Native Americans were certain that a race of apelike animals had been living in the neighboring mountain for centuries. They called these creatures Sasquatch.

Hence, the correct option is (C).

21. "Globalization is often seen, both in journalistic discussions and in remarkably many academic writings, as a process of westernization."

Upon perusal of the above statement, it can be concluded that globalization is perceived often by media and academia as a process of Westernisation.

Hence, the correct option is (C).

22. "There is a strong need to separate out the different questions that appear merged together in the rhetoric of the antiglobalization protests. The globalization of knowledge deserves a particularly high profile recognition, despite all the good things that can be rightly said about the importance of "Local knowledge"."

Upon perusal of the above statement, it can be concluded that the author encourages an unbiased evaluation of globalization and not an unconditioned rejection of globalization.

Hence, the correct option is (D)

23. "Even though globalization is one of the most discussed topics in the contemporary world. It is not altogether a well-defined concept."

Upon perusal of the above statements, it can be concluded that globalization is not a well-defined concept.

Hence, the correct option is (C).

24. "A wholesale rejection of globalization would not only go against global business, but it would also cut out movements of ideas, understanding, and knowledge that can help all the people of the world, including the most disadvantaged members of the world population."

Upon perusal of the above statement, it can be concluded that only the statements (a) and (b) are correct.

Hence, the correct option is (A).

25. "A comprehensive rejection of globalization can thus be powerfully counterproductive."

Upon perusal of the above statement, it can be concluded that wholesale rejection of globalization is counterproductive.

Hence, the correct option is (B).

26. The given passage is about the golf player Matsuyama and how he won the Master's championship.

Destroyed(verb): To damage something so badly that it cannot be used.

Conserved(verb): To keep and protect something from damage, change, or waste.

From the above line, we can say that: Conserved is the opposite word of the destroyed.

Hence, the correct option is (B).

27. The given passage is about the golf player Matsuyama and how he won the Master's championship.

Let us refer to the passage - He did not want to take part, but in the end, he decided that he would play. He wanted to make Japanese people happy again.

From the above line, we can say that: To make Japanese people happy again.

Hence, the correct option is (B).

28. The given passage is about the golf player Matsuyama and how he won the Master's championship.

Let us refer to the passage - He became the first Japanese man and the first Asian man in history to win. He won only by one shot over Will Zalatoris from the US.

From the above line, we can say that: Matsuyama won from Will Zaltoris in Masters.

Hence, the correct option is (A).

29. The given passage is about the golf player Matsuyama and how he won the Master's championship.

Let us refer to the passage - He wanted to make Japanese people happy again. In April 2021, he made Japanese people even happier when he won the Masters for the first time.

From the above line, we can say that: In the year 2021 Matsuyama won the Masters.

Hence, the correct option is (B).

30. The given passage is about the golf player Matsuyama and how he won the Master's championship.

Let us refer to the passage - Hideki Matsuyama was born in 1992. His father introduced him to golf when Matsuyama was only four years old.

From the above line, we can say that: At the age of four Matsuyama's father introduced him to golf.

Hence, the correct option is (D).

Ques (1-30):Direction: Select the most appropriate option to improve the underlined segment in the given sentence. If there is no need to improve it, select 'No improvement'.

Q.1 A hole is in my pocket.

A. There is a hole **B.** A hole there is
C. A hole are there **D.** No improvement

Q.2 Many a person are unable of distinguish right from wrong.

A. are unable to **B.** is unable to
C. are capable of **D.** No improvement

Q.3 If you had asked me, I had told you not to invest in that property.

A. I will tell you
B. I would tell you
C. I would have told you
D. No improvement

Q.4 She are having two brothers and three sisters.

A. is having **B.** has
C. No improvement **D.** have

Q.5 I am not use to drink coffee.

A. No improvement **B.** not used to drinking
C. not use to drank **D.** not used to drink

Q.6 I suggest you to see a solicitor.

A. am suggesting you **B.** suggest that you
C. No improvement **D.** suggest you that

Q.7 I will not go to the party lest you will promise to accompany me.

A. until you should **B.** if you will
C. No improvement **D.** unless you

Q.8 We are coping the problems with the best of our ability.

A. No improvement
B. coping with the problems to
C. coping the problems at
D. coping in the problems by

Q.9 I am really looking forward to meet you.

A. No improvement **B.** to be meeting you
C. to have met you **D.** to meeting you

Q.10 The child put a ladder on the wall and climbed up.

A. No improvement **B.** against the wall
C. above the wall **D.** over a wall

Q.11 The place was not cold only and also damp.

A. only cold not also
B. No improvement
C. not only cold but also
D. not only cold and both

Q.12 There was an argument about if we shall move to another city.

A. about if we should move
B. on if we shall be moving
C. about whether we should move
D. No improvement

Q.13 I will accept the responsibility while a time comes.

A. until a time **B.** when the time
C. No improvement **D.** whenever a time

Q.14 This stain can be remove by lime juice.

A. removed with **B.** remove from
C. No improvement **D.** removed through

Q.15 She is not ready for marriage, isn't it?

A. is she **B.** is it
C. No improvement **D.** isn't she

Q.16 I bet you can't beat me by chess.

A. at chess **B.** in the chess
C. No improvement **D.** on chess

Q.17 He has being put behind prison for life.

A. No improvement **B.** been put behind
C. being putting in **D.** been put in

Q.18 He was considered a genius by his school headmaster.

A. was been considered
B. was to be considered
C. was considering
D. No improvement

Q.19 Why not you to be a good boy and sit down?

A. don't you be **B.** you are not being
C. No improvement **D.** you not be

Q.20 You have not showed any improvement in your handwriting.

A. No improvement **B.** has not shown
C. have not shown **D.** had not showed

Q.21 I have been working with children before, so I know what to expect.

A. have worked **B.** am working
C. work **D.** No improvement

Q.22 I was being depressed when you called.

A. being depressing **B.** feeling depressed
C. No improvement **D.** going depressed

Q.23 Our cook puts too many salt in the food.

A. No improvement **B.** Putting too much
C. Puts too much **D.** Puts very much

Q.24 Riya went into the shop because it has sale.

A. No improvement
B. it is having sale
C. it having a sale
D. it had a sale

Q.25 You have to wear this uniform whether you likes it or not.

A. whether you like it or not
B. whether you are liking it or not
C. No improvement
D. Whether if you like it or not

Q.26 You have my mobile number, isn't it?

A. don't you
B. No improvement
C. do you
D. has you

Q.27 Many people have become aware of the advantages of preventive health care nowadays.

A. are become aware of
B. will be becoming aware to
C. have becoming aware for
D. No improvement

Q.28 The milk has boiled over and falling onto the stove.

A. falls into the stove
B. fallen onto the stove
C. No improvement
D. fall over in the stove

Q.29 It has been raining very hardly since morning.

A. is been raining very hardly
B. No improvement
C. has been raining very hard
D. have been raining very hardly

Q.30 Dinesh requested the lady at the counter to give him a seat besides the window.

A. No improvement
B. a seat beside the window
C. an seat beside a window
D. one seat besides the window

// Smart Answer Sheet //

Correct Indicates percentage of students who answered questions correctly.

Skipped Indicates percentage of students who skipped questions.

Q.	Ans.	Correct	Skipped
1	A	87.02 %	10.14 %
2	B	83.75 %	12.03 %
3	C	88.33 %	10.4 %
4	B	89.33 %	10.62 %
5	B	83.77 %	12.87 %
6	B	76.22 %	18.17 %
7	D	85.71 %	11.39 %
8	B	79.87 %	16.39 %
9	D	79.45 %	20.28 %
10	B	76.1 %	18.24 %
11	C	79.97 %	15.17 %
12	C	84.47 %	10.47 %
13	B	86.54 %	10.07 %
14	A	80.7 %	11.08 %
15	A	77.95 %	11.2 %
16	A	79.46 %	13.62 %
17	D	79.92 %	18.6 %
18	D	80.21 %	17.6 %
19	A	79.92 %	12.86 %
20	C	83.31 %	15.8 %
21	A	78.16 %	12.72 %
22	B	77.12 %	22.68 %
23	C	86.86 %	12.0 %
24	D	82.57 %	14.35 %
25	A	84.02 %	15.22 %
26	A	76.11 %	22.4 %
27	D	88.84 %	10.21 %
28	B	86.44 %	13.01 %
29	C	76.37 %	12.29 %
30	B	84.86 %	13.2 %

Performance Analysis	
Avg. Score (%)	43.33%
Toppers Score (%)	60.0%
Your Score	

//Hints and Solutions//

1. The correct sentence is- 'There is a hole in my pocket.'

The adverb 'there' is used to introduce the subject of a sentence, especially before the verbs be, seem, and appear.

Example:

There seemed to be a problem with finding a date for the meeting.

Hence, the correct option is (A).

2. The correct sentence is- 'Many a person is unable to distinguish right from wrong.'

In the case of the following words, the verbs used will be singular:

Each, every/everyone, someone/somebody, none/ nobody, one, any, many a, more than one, etc.

For example:

Everyone are addicted to smartphones nowadays. (incorrect)

Everyone is addicted to smartphones nowadays. (correct)

Hence, the correct option is (B).

3. The correct answer is- I would have told you.

Conditional sentences are statements discussing known factors or hypothetical situations and their consequences. One of the structures is mentioned below:

This particular type is followed when something didn't happen as a certain condition wasn't fulfilled.

If + Subject + had + V3 + object, Subject + Would have + V3 + Object.

For example:

If I had noticed you, I would had call you. (incorrect)

If I had noticed you, I would have called you. (correct)

Hence, the correct option is (C).

4. The correct sentence is- 'She has two brothers and three sisters.'

Certain verbs used only in the simple present tense are given below:

- See, think, know, has/have, possess, like, want, desire, hate, seem, imagine, etc.

Example:

- My brother is owning a car. (incorrect)
- My brother owns a car. (correct)

We need a verb that shows possession, the verb 'has' will be the correct choice.

Hence, the correct option is (B).

5. The correct answer is- not used to drinking.

The verbs/adjectives/phrases given below are followed by 'V1 + ing':

with a view to, addicted to, used to, before, given/taken to, prone to, in addition to, look forward to, owing to, etc.

Hence, the correct option is (B).

6. I suggest that you see a solicitor.

The given sentence is an example of indirect speech form as there are no comma and inverted commas. In that case, the verb 'suggest' will be followed by the conjunction 'that'.

Hence, the correct option is (B).

7. The correct answer is "unless you".

In the given sentence, the use of the conjunction 'lest' is incorrect. The conjunction 'lest' means with the intention of preventing something undesirable; to avoid the risk of. The conjunction 'unless' should be used in place of 'lest' as per the context of the sentence. The conjunction 'unless' means except if (used to introduce the case in which a statement being made is not true or valid).

'Unless' is followed by a present tense, a past tense, or a past perfect tense (never by a conditional). The given sentence is the first conditional sentence, therefore the format should be unless + present tense. Therefore, the use of the verb 'will' is superfluous and it should be removed from the sentence.

Correct sentence: I will not go to the party unless you promise to accompany me.

Hence, the correct option is (D).

8. We are coping with the problems to the best of our ability.

The verb 'cope' in the given sentence an intransitive verb meaning to deal with something well, despite or in the face of some difficulty. The verb 'cope' is usually followed by the preposition 'with'. The given sentence is in the present continuous tense, therefore, the present participle "coping with" should be used.

The present participle verb "coping with" means to deal with something usually skillfully or efficiently. Also, in the underlined segment, the use of the preposition 'with' is incorrect. The particle 'to' should be used in place of the preposition 'with'.

'To' here is used for indicating a proposition that is known, believed, or reported about a specified person or thing.

Hence, the correct option is (B).

9. I am really looking forward to meeting you.

In the given sentence, the preposition 'to' is a part of the phrasal verb "looking forward to" (verb + adverb + preposition).

The subject in the sentence is 'I', the verb in the sentence is "am really looking forward to" and the object is "meet you".

But in the object of a sentence, the verbs are never used and only the nouns, pronouns or the noun phrases are used.

In the underlined segment, the word 'meet' is a verb and a gerund (here, meeting) should be used in place of the verb 'meet'.

Hence, the correct option is (D).

10. The correct answer is "against the wall".

In the given sentence, the use of the preposition 'on' is incorrect. The preposition 'on' means physically in contact with and supported by a surface.

The preposition 'against' means in or into physical contact with something, so as to be supported by or collide with it.

The correct sentence is- The child put a ladder against the wall and climbed up.

Hence, the correct option is (B).

11. The place was not only cold but also damp.

In the given sentence, the position of the adverb 'only' after the adjective 'cold' is incorrect.

We use only as an adverb to mean that something is limited to some people, things, an amount, or an activity:

Also, the use of the conjunction 'and' in the given sentence is inappropriate.

The conjunction 'and' means in addition to

The correlative conjunction "Not only, but also" is used for emphasizing the fact that there is something more to add.

Hence, the correct option is (C).

12. There was an argument about whether we should move to another city.

In the given sentence, the use of the conjunction 'if' is incorrect. The conjunction 'if' is used to introduce a condition (something that must be satisfied before something else occurs). The conjunction 'whether' is used for expressing a doubt or choice between alternatives. Therefore, the conjunction 'whether' should be used in place of the conjunction 'if'.

Also, the form of the verb 'shall' is incorrect in the underlined segment as the given sentence is in the past tense. Therefore, the past tense form of the verb 'should' be used in place of the base form of the verb 'shall'.

Hence, the correct option is (C).

13. The correct sentence is, "I will accept the responsibility when the time comes."

In the given sentence, the use of the adverb 'while' and the use of the indefinite article 'a' is incorrect.

The adverb 'while' means during which. The adverb 'when' should be used in place of 'while'. The adverb 'when' means at or on which (referring to a time or circumstance).

Also, the use of the article 'a' before the noun 'time' is incorrect as "a time" is used when describing a period of time. As the noun 'time' is specific, therefore the definite article 'the' should be used. The definite article 'the' is used to describe a specific noun, whereas the indefinite articles 'a/an' is used to describe a more general noun.

Hence, the correct option is (B).

14. The correct sentence is, "This stain can be removed with lime juice."

In the given sentence, the use of the form of the verb 'remove' and the preposition 'by' are incorrect. The given sentence is showing a general possibility, therefore, the past participle form of the verb 'removed' should be used here.

Also, the preposition 'by' is used for indicating the means of achieving something. The preposition 'with' should be used in place of 'by' as it is used for indicating the material used for a purpose.

Hence, the correct option is (A).

15. The correct sentence is, "She is not ready for marriage, is she?"

The given sentence is a negative statement and having a tag question. The basic structure of a tag question is a positive statement + negative tag & negative statement + positive tag.

The auxiliary verb from the positive statement is repeated in the tag and changed to negative.

The auxiliary verb from the negative statement is repeated in the tag and changed to positive.

In the given sentence, the statement is negative, therefore, it will take a positive tag.

Also, the pronoun 'it' is used to refer to a thing while the pronoun 'she' is used for referring to a woman, girl, or female animal. Therefore, "is she" should be used in place of "isn't it".

Hence, the correct option is (A).

16. The correct Sentence is, "I bet you can't beat me at chess."

In the given sentence, the use of the preposition 'by' is incorrect. The preposition 'by' is used for indicating the means of achieving something.

Beat somebody (at something) means to defeat someone in a game or competition. So 'by' should be replaced by 'at'.

Hence, the correct option is (A).

17. The correct Sentence is, "He has been put in prison for life."

In the given sentence, the use of the present participle form of the verb 'being' and the preposition 'behind' is incorrect.

The given sentence is in the present perfect continuous tense, therefore the past participle form of the verb 'been' should be used.

The present perfect continuous tense structure: auxiliary verb 'have/has' (present tense) + auxiliary 'be' (past participle) + main verb (past participle V_3).

Also, the preposition 'behind' means at or to the far side of (something), typically so as to be hidden by it.

The preposition 'in' should be used in place of 'behind' as it is used for expressing the situation of something that is or appears to be enclosed or surrounded by something else.

Hence, the correct option is (D).

18. The correct answer is- 'No improvement'.

The given sentence is an example of Passive Voice. Here, 'was considered' is rightly used. Because the structure of it is:

Subject (Objective Case)+was/were+V_3+Object(Subjective Case).

Hence, the correct option is (D).

19. The correct sentence is- 'Why don't you be a good boy and sit down?'

We know that after the question word 'Why' we should use an auxiliary verb. After 'Why' we should use the auxiliary verb 'do'. The structure of these kinds of sentences is as follows:

Why + auxiliary verb + subject + main verb?

Example: When does the movie start?

In the given question 'not' is used which is grammatically incorrect. Whereas, it should be 'don't you'. Here, 'to' is also used incorrectly. It should be removed.

Hence, the correct option is (A).

20. The correct sentence is- 'You have not shown any improvement in your handwriting.'

The given sentence is an example of the present perfect tense. Its structure is as follows:

Subject + Has/Have + V3.

The third form (past participle form) of 'show' is 'shown'.

Hence, the correct option is (C).

21. The correct sentence is- 'I have worked with children before, so I know what to expect.'

Here, 'have been working' is wrongly used because we know that the present perfect continuous tense is used when we talk about an action that began in the past and continues in the present. And may also continue in the future.

Here, the given sentence is not continuous. And the action is no longer being performed. So, the tense cannot be the present continuous tense ('am working') or simple present tense ('work')

Hence, the correct option is (A).

22. The correct sentence is- 'I was feeling depressed when you called.'

Here, the sentence is conveying a short momentary state of mind. The word being is used when we are conveying something that has been existing for a long time, a considerable duration.

'Feeling' is something that happens for a short span of time, momentarily. So, 'Feeling' is the most appropriate word.

'Being depressing' and 'going depressed' is incorrect because:

- The former indicates that the person was causing someone else to be depressed.
- The latter is grammatically incorrect.

Hence, the correct option is (B).

23. The subject of the sentence 'our cook' is a singular subject.

- So, it will take a singular verb i.e., puts.
- 'Puts' is used with third person singular noun.
- So, it is correctly used.

'Many' is used with countable nouns and 'much' is used with uncountable nouns.

For Examples:

- How much petrol is in the car?
- How many people were at the meeting?
- Here 'salt' is uncountable, so we will use 'much'.

Therefore, the correct sentence is "Our cook puts too much salt in the food".

Hence, the correct option is (C).

24. The correct sentence is: "Riya went into the shop because it had a sale."

The error lies in 'it has sale'.

- The sentence is in the past tense. The action has already happened.
- The word 'went' indicates that the sentence is in past tense and past tense form of 'has' is 'had'.
- Article 'a' is used before indefinite things.

Hence, the correct option is (D).

25. whether you like it or not is the correct answer.

'Likes' is used with the third person singular noun like he or she.

With the second person pronoun, we use the base form of the verb i.e., like.

Hence, the correct option is (A).

26. The correct sentence: You have my mobile number, don't you?

The underlined phrase is a question tag.

A positive statement is followed by a negative question tag. Example: Jack is from Spain, isn't he?

Mary can speak English, can't she?

A negative statement is followed by a positive question tag. Example: They aren't funny, are they?

He shouldn't say things like that, should he?

Since, the sentence is positive, the question tag should be negative so we can reject options (C) and (D).

'It' is used while referring to a thing. Example: I like your jacket. Is it new? Here, 'it' is referring to 'jacket'.

Here, the speaker is referring to a person i.e., you.

Hence, the correct option is (A).

27. No Improvement is needed in the above sentence.

'Nowadays' is used which means the speaker is talking about the days which are ongoing at the present.

So, we need to use the present perfect tense.

Option (A) is in the simple present tense.

Option (B) is in the future continuous tense.

Option (C) uses 'have' which is incorrect.

Hence, the correct option is (D).

28. The milk has boiled over and fallen onto the stove.

The sentence is in the present perfect tense as indicated by the words 'has boiled'. So, we will use the past participle form of verb i.e., fallen.

Onto means moving to a location on the surface.

'Into' means expressing movement or action with the result that someone or something becomes enclosed or surrounded by something else.

Over means extending directly upwards from.

Hence, the correct option is (B).

29. It has been raining very hardly since morning.

The word 'since' is used which means that the sentence is highlighting an event that has begun from a time in the past. So, the use of 'has' is correct.

'hardly' means scarcely which is incorrectly used. Instead of 'hardly', 'hard' must be used which means that it was raining heavily.

Hence, the correct option is (C).

30. The correct sentence will be:

"Dinesh requested the lady at the counter to give him a seat beside the window."

Since, 'seat' starts with a consonant, so the use of 'a' is correct.

'Beside' means 'at the side of'.

'Besides' mean 'in addition to something'.

Here, beside must be used as the sentence talks about the location.

Hence, the correct option is (B).

Q.1 In the following question, four words are given out of which one word is correctly spelt. Select the correctly spelt word.

A. Repositary **B.** Repository
C. Repozitory **D.** Repozitary

Q.2 Select the wrongly spelt word.

A. Transgresser **B.** Accommodate
C. Perspicuous **D.** Assassin

Q.3 In the following question, four words are given out of which one word is correctly spelt. Select the correctly spelt word.

A. Especally **B.** Especially
C. Especialy **D.** Espesially

Q.4 In the following question, four words are given out of which one word is correctly spelt. Select the correctly spelt word.

A. Privarticate **B.** Prevaricate
C. Pervaticate **D.** Pervarticate

Q.5 Select the wrongly spelt word.

A. Summarize **B.** Reidiculous
C. Receptionist **D.** Inhuman

Q.6 Identify the word that is spelt correctly.

[Allahabad High Court Review Officer (RO), 2019]

A. Conscientiuous **B.** Consientious
C. Conscientious **D.** Consceintious

Q.7 In the following question, four words are given out of which one word is correctly spelt. Select the correctly spelt word.

A. Embaras **B.** Embarass
C. Embarrass **D.** Embarrase

Q.8 Which among the following is the correct spelling according to the dictionary?

[Allahabad High Court Review Officer (RO), 2019]

A. Millenieum **B.** Milennieum
C. Millennium **D.** Mileniumm

Q.9 Identify the word that is spelt correctly.

[Allahabad High Court Review Officer (RO), 2019]

A. Baleweather **B.** Ballwether
C. Bellwether **D.** Belwether

Q.10 Select the wrongly spelt word.

A. Germinate **B.** Geometry
C. Generalise **D.** Geniune

Q.11 In the following question, four words are given out of which one word is correctly spelt. Select the correctly spelt word.

A. Exprimant **B.** Experriment
C. Experment **D.** Experiment

Q.12 Select the wrongly spelt word.

[SSC Sub Inspector (CPO), 2020]

A. Presure **B.** Electric
C. Central **D.** Irrigation

Q.13 In the following question, four words are given out of which one word is correctly spelt. Select the correctly spelt word.

A. Transgresser **B.** Transgressor
C. Transgressar **D.** Transgressr

Q.14 In the following question, four words are given out of which one word is correctly spelt. Select the correctly spelt word.

A. Optsion **B.** Opsion **C.** Option **D.** Optshon

Q.15 In the following question, four words are given out of which one word is correctly spelt. Select the correctly spelt word.

A. Refrence **B.** Reference
C. Referense **D.** Refference

Q.16 Select the wrongly spelt word.

A. Absense **B.** Acquiesce
C. Acquisition **D.** Acquit

Q.17 In the following question, four words are given out of which one word is correctly spelt. Select the correctly spelt word.

A. Apparent **B.** Appearent
C. Apearent **D.** Apearrent

Q.18 Select the wrongly spelt word.

A. Argument **B.** Ignorant
C. Conscience **D.** Appearent

Q.19 Select the correctly spelt word.

A. Ilogical **B.** Achieve
C. Appearence **D.** Grammer

Q.20 Find out that word, the spelling of which is wrong.

A. Immunity **B.** Immaculate
C. Imminent **D.** Immitate

Q.21 Find out that word, the spelling of which is wrong.

A. Sargeant **B.** Shallot **C.** Shackle **D.** Shellac

Q.22 Find out that word, the spelling of which is wrong.

A. Beetle **B.** Beautician
C. Bearable **D.** Beautifull

Q.23 Find out that word, the spelling of which is wrong.

A. Anxiety **B.** Ankel

C. Accommodation D. Allergy

Q.24 Find out that word, the spelling of which is wrong.

A. Recuperate B. Pasture
C. Populace D. Penence

Q.25 Find out that word, the spelling of which is wrong.

A. Shutter B. Silhoutte
C. Shepherd D. Shield

Q.26 Select the wrongly spelt word.

[SSC Sub Inspector (CPO), 2020]

A. Custody B. Custom C. Cursory D. Curtesy

Q.27 Select the wrongly spelt word.

[SSC Sub Inspector (CPO), 2020]

A. Laboratary B. Boundary
C. Olfactory D. Elementary

Q.28 Select the wrongly spelt word.

[SSC Sub Inspector (CPO), 2020]

A. Decibel B. Decease C. Decency D. Decieve

Q.29 Select the wrongly spelt word.

A. Fastedious B. Fashion
C. Fascination D. Fascism

Q.30 Select the wrongly spelt word.

[SSC Sub Inspector (CPO), 2020]

A. Midget B. Migraine C. Migrent D. Militant

// Smart Answer Sheet //

Correct — Indicates percentage of students who answered questions correctly.

Skipped — Indicates percentage of students who skipped questions.

Q.	Ans.	Correct	Skipped
1	B	89.22 %	10.23 %
2	A	89.5 %	10.04 %
3	B	79.92 %	11.15 %
4	B	76.81 %	19.73 %
5	B	82.61 %	13.71 %
6	C	87.47 %	11.43 %
7	C	83.24 %	12.97 %
8	C	79.94 %	16.17 %
9	C	85.35 %	13.62 %
10	D	76.37 %	21.44 %
11	D	85.66 %	12.03 %
12	A	87.93 %	11.45 %
13	B	84.72 %	14.69 %
14	C	83.25 %	16.46 %
15	B	87.99 %	10.48 %
16	A	85.72 %	12.32 %
17	A	79.74 %	10.44 %
18	D	81.28 %	11.1 %
19	B	84.08 %	14.31 %
20	D	81.89 %	11.63 %
21	A	77.23 %	17.67 %
22	D	89.76 %	10.16 %
23	B	78.18 %	18.13 %
24	D	76.58 %	15.27 %
25	B	88.34 %	10.92 %
26	D	84.49 %	13.01 %
27	A	83.34 %	10.48 %
28	D	86.73 %	11.42 %
29	A	84.32 %	15.14 %
30	C	83.69 %	14.06 %

Performance Analysis	
Avg. Score (%)	56.67%
Toppers Score (%)	66.67%
Your Score	

//Hints and Solutions//

1. Repository is the correctly spelt word.

Repository: a place where things are stored and can be found

Hence, the correct option is (B).

2. Transgresser is the wrongly spelt word. The correct word is Transgressor. It means 'a person who breaks a law or moral rule'.

Hence, the correct option is (A).

3. Especially is the correctly spelt word.

Especially: used to single out one person or thing over all others.

Hence, the correct option is (B).

4. Prevaricate is the correctly spelt word.

Prevaricate: speak or act in an evasive way

Hence, the correct option is (B).

5. Reidiculous is the wrongly spelt word. The correct word is Ridiculous. It means deserving or inviting derision or mockery; absurd.

Hence, the correct option is (B).

6. Conscientious is the correctly spelt word.

Conscientious (adjective): Putting a lot of effort into your work. For example: She was a conscientious worker, and I'll miss her.

Hence, the correct option is (C).

7. Embarrass is the correctly spelt word.

Embarrass(verb): To cause someone to feel nervous, worried, or uncomfortable.

Hence, the correct option is (C).

8. The correct spelling according to the dictionary is Millennium.

Millennium(noun): A millennium is a period of one thousand years, especially one which begins and ends with a year ending in '000', for example, the period from the year 1000 to the year 2000.

Hence, the correct option is (C).

9. Bellwether (noun): Someone or something that shows how a situation will develop or change.

For example:

- Investors will be eagerly awaiting guidance from bellwether stocks.
- The report is viewed as a bellwether for national economic trends.

Hence, the correct option is (C).

10. Let us explore the options:

- 'Geniune': There is no such word in the English language or we can say that there is some spelling mistake in this word. However, if we interchange the position of the letters 'i' and 'u' then it will become a meaningful word 'Genuine' which means truly what something is said to be; authentic
- 'Germinate' means to come into existence and develop.
- 'Geometry' means the shape and relative arrangement of the parts of something.
- 'Generalise' means to make something more widespread or widely applicable.

So, the correct spelling of the wrongly spelt words is "Genuine".

'Generalise' is also spelt as 'generalize'. The former is the accepted British spelling while the latter is the Americanized version.

Hence, the correct option is (D).

11. Experiment is the correctly spelt word.

'Experiment' means to try out new ideas or methods.

Hence, the correct option is (D).

12. 'Presure': There is no such word in English or we can say that there is some spelling mistake in this word, correct spelling is 'Pressure'.

'Pressure' means continuous physical force exerted on or against an object by something in contact with it.

Hence, the correct option is (A).

13. Transgressor is the correctly spelt word.

Transgressor: a person who breaks a law or moral rule.

Hence, the correct option is (B).

14. Option is the correctly spelt word.

Option: a thing that is or may be chosen

Hence, the correct option is (C).

15. Reference is the correctly spelt word.

'Reference' means the action of mentioning or alluding to something.

Hence, the correct option is (B).

16. Absense is the wrongly spelt word. The correct spelling is 'Absence'.

Absence - the fact of something/somebody not being there; lack.

Example: In the absence of a doctor, try to help the injured person yourself.

Hence, the correct option is (A).

17. Apparent is the correctly spelt word.

Apparent - clearly visible or understood; obvious.

Hence, the correct option is (A).

18. Appearent is the wrongly spelt word. The correct spelling is Apparent.

Apparent - clearly visible or understood; obvious.

Example: She laughed for no apparent reason.

Hence, the correct option is (D).

19. Out of all the options, only 'Achieve' is correctly spelt.

Achieve - to gain something, usually by effort or skill.

Example: You have achieved the success you deserve.

Hence, the correct option is (B).

20. Immitate is the wrongly spelt word. The correct spelling is Imitate.

Imitate: take or follow as a model.

Hence, the correct option is (D).

21. Sargeant is the wrongly spelt word. The correct spelling is Sergeant.

Sergeant is a rank in many uniformed organizations, principally military and policing forces.

Hence, the correct option is (A).

22. Beautifull is the wrongly spelt word. The correct spelling is Beautiful.

Beautiful: pleasing the senses or mind aesthetically.

Hence, the correct option is (D).

23. Ankel is the wrongly spelt word. The correct spelling is Ankle.

The ankle is a large joint made up of three bones: The shin bone (tibia) The thinner bone running next to the shin bone (fibula) A foot bone that sits above the heel bone (talus).

Hence, the correct option is (B).

24. Penence is the wrongly spelt word. The correct spelling is Penance.

Penance: punishment inflicted on oneself as an outward expression of repentance for wrongdoing.

Hence, the correct option is (D).

25. Silhoutte is the wrongly spelt word. The correct spelling is Silhouette.

Silhouette: the dark shape and outline of someone or something visible in restricted light against a brighter background.

Hence, the correct option is (B).

26. The correct answer is 'curtesy'.

Courtesy: Polite and pleasant behaviour that shows respect for other people

Example: His abilities, his courtesy and his upright character made him a universal favourite.

Hence, the correct option is (D).

27. The correct answer is 'laboratary'.

'Laboratary': There is no such word in English or we can say that there is some spelling mistake in this word, correct spelling is 'Laboratory'.

Laboratory: a room or building that is used for scientific research, testing, experiments, etc. or for teaching about science

Example: The blood will be tested by a laboratory technician.

Hence, the correct option is (A).

28. The correct answer is 'decieve'.

'Decieve': There is no such word in English or we can say that there is some spelling mistake in this word, correct spelling is 'Deceive'

Deceive: to try to make somebody believe something that is not true

Example: If you're no longer engaged, why do you have to deceive him?

Hence, the correct option is (D).

29. The correct answer is 'fastedious'.

'Fastedious': There is no such word in English or we can say that there is some spelling mistake in this word, correct spelling is 'Fastidious'.

Fastidious: difficult to please; wanting everything to be perfect

Example: he was too fastidious to do anything that might get her dirty.

Hence, the correct option is (A).

30. The correct answer is 'migrent'.

'Migrent': There is no such word in English or we can say that there is some spelling mistake in this word, correct spelling is 'Migrant'.

Migrant: a person who moves from place to place looking for work

Example: Many migrant workers are Chinese and the language is widely read and spoken there.

Hence, the correct option is (C).

Ques (1-25):Direction: Identify the segment in the sentence which contains a grammatical error.

Q.1 Neither Sam nor I are interested in attending the meeting.

A. Neither Sam nor I **B.** are interested
C. in attending **D.** the meeting

Q.2 Laws and rules are made to safeguarding our rights and protect us.

A. Safeguarding our rights
B. Laws and rules
C. Are made to
D. Are protect us

Q.3 Poor people have run down of food supplies during the lockdown.

A. during the lockdown
B. Poor people have
C. run down of
D. food supplies

Q.4 The small cafe at the end of the road is her.

A. of the road **B.** is her
C. at the end **D.** The small cafe

Q.5 He loses his tempers on the slightest provocation.

A. He loses **B.** His tempers on
C. The slightest **D.** Provocation

Q.6 The man played the flute and led all the mouse out of the town.

A. Out of the town **B.** The flute and led
C. The man played **D.** All the mouse

Q.7 I didn't knew you had gone to Goa for a vacation.

A. for a vacation **B.** you had gone
C. to Goa **D.** I didn't knew

Q.8 We must plan how can we cope with the present situation.

A. Cope with the **B.** We must plan
C. How can we **D.** Present situation

Q.9 I want you to complete this work by two days.

A. by two days **B.** I want you
C. this work **D.** to complete

Q.10 You must be careful about what you say as you meet her.

A. as you **B.** meet her
C. about what you say **D.** You must be careful

Q.11 Although this is a narrowest street, many large trucks can enter it.

A. many large trucks **B.** Although this is
C. can enter it **D.** a narrowest street

Q.12 Zoya won the first prize in the race unless she stumbled and fell.

A. stumbled and fell **B.** Zoya won the first
C. prize in the race **D.** unless she

Q.13 Do you mind lending me your book for a hour?

A. your book **B.** for a hour
C. Do you mind **D.** lending me

Q.14 This jewellery box is made from silver and is an antique piece.

A. This jewellery box **B.** an antique piece
C. and is **D.** is made from silver

Q.15 There was enough evidence to convict him on selling of fake medicines.

A. on selling of
B. fake medicines
C. There was enough evidence
D. to convict him

Q.16 The tired and vexed travellers waiting at the airport for a long time.

A. waiting at the airport
B. vexed travellers
C. The tired and
D. for a long time

Q.17 The venue for the wedding have not been finalized yet.

A. for the wedding **B.** The venue
C. have not **D.** been finalised yet

Q.18 She has been a member of this club since it's formation.

A. this club **B.** since it's formation
C. She has been **D.** a member of

Q.19 No one of them come to the inauguration of our new factory.

A. come to the **B.** No one of them
C. inauguration of **D.** our new factory

Q.20 The three of them shouted out to each another when the train started moving.

A. The three of them
B. when the train
C. shouted out to each another
D. started moving

Q.21 A closed economy is identified as a human community that produces all it consumes and consumed all it produces.

A. A closed economy is identified
B. as a human community
C. that produces all it consumes
D. and consumed all it produces

Q.22 Iron is the most useful against all metals.

A. Iron is **B.** the most useful

C. against all metals **D.** No error

Q.23 While every care have been taken in preparing the results, the company reserves the right to correct any inadvertent errors at a later stage.

A. While every care have been taken
B. in preparing the results,
C. the company reserves the right to correct
D. any inadvertent errors at a later stage

Q.24 My sister and me are planning a trip from Jaipur to Delhi.

A. My sister and me are
B. planning a trip
C. from Jaipur to Delhi
D. No error

Q.25 Despite the thrill of winning the lottery last week, my neighbour still seems happily.

A. Despite the thrill of winning
B. the lottery last week,
C. my neighbour
D. still seems happily

Ques (26-30):Direction: Given below is a sentence that has multiple parts. Find out the error/ no error and indicate your response accordingly.

Q.26 Children are not allowed to use the swimming pool unless they are with an adult.

A. Children are not allowed
B. to use the swimming pool
C. unless they are with an adult
D. No error

Q.27 Her knowledge of Indian languages are far beyond the common.

A. Her knowledge
B. of Indian languages
C. are far beyond the common
D. No error

Q.28 You look as if you have ran all the way home.

A. You look as if **B.** you have ran
C. all the way home **D.** No error

Q.29 The real voyage of discovery consist not in seeking new landscapes, but in having new eyes.

A. The real voyage of discovery
B. consist not in seeking new landscapes
C. but in having new eyes
D. No error

Q.30 No struggle can ever succeeded without women participating side by side with men.

A. No struggle can ever succeeded
B. without women participating
C. side by side with men
D. No error

// Smart Answer Sheet //

Correct — Indicates percentage of students who answered questions correctly.

Skipped — Indicates percentage of students who skipped questions.

Q.	Ans.	Correct	Skipped
1	B	87.44 %	11.41 %
2	A	89.54 %	10.29 %
3	C	86.09 %	10.44 %
4	B	81.11 %	11.74 %
5	B	85.34 %	10.46 %
6	D	82.91 %	10.64 %
7	D	84.77 %	12.96 %
8	C	76.34 %	13.31 %
9	A	89.66 %	10.11 %
10	A	79.5 %	11.78 %
11	D	87.9 %	11.22 %
12	D	84.1 %	11.52 %
13	B	82.08 %	13.86 %
14	D	88.95 %	10.87 %
15	A	76.45 %	17.19 %
16	A	80.94 %	14.07 %
17	C	81.53 %	15.48 %
18	B	82.9 %	10.85 %
19	A	86.89 %	10.83 %
20	C	87.82 %	11.44 %
21	D	78.07 %	21.57 %
22	C	78.04 %	20.02 %
23	A	85.15 %	13.73 %
24	A	85.96 %	12.06 %
25	D	83.77 %	15.33 %
26	D	86.67 %	11.01 %
27	C	76.55 %	11.59 %
28	B	79.75 %	15.05 %
29	B	76.5 %	16.82 %
30	A	82.28 %	17.47 %

Performance Analysis	
Avg. Score (%)	36.67%
Toppers Score (%)	53.33%
Your Score	

//Hints and Solutions//

1. 'Neither Sam nor I **am** interested in attending the meeting.'

If the main subject is followed by the following words/phrases, the verb will conform to the nearest subject: Neither-nor, either-or, not only-but also, none but, nor, or, etc.

Example:

Either Sam or Eric are coming to the wedding. (incorrect)

Either Sam or Eric is coming to the wedding. (correct)

Hence, the correct option is (B).

2. The correct answer is- 'safeguarding our rights.'

A to-infinitive is the 'to + the base form of the verb', for example, to sing, to dance, etc. There are certain verbs that are used in a particular pattern given below:

Subject + verb + noun/pronoun + to-infinitive.

Example:

I urge you helping me solve this problem. (incorrect)

I urge you to help me solve this problem. (correct)

So, the correct sentence is- 'Laws and rules are made to safeguard our rights and protect us.'

Hence, the correct option is (A).

3. The correct answer is- 'run down of.'

The meanings of the phrasal verb: run down - criticize, disparage

As per the context of the sentence, the poor didn't have any food left during the lockdown. The phrasal verb 'run out of' will be the correct choice in the 3rd part of the sentence.

Hence, the correct option is (C).

4. The correct answer is- is her.

Independent possessive pronouns (also called absolute possessive pronouns) must be used without a noun.

Correct Sentence: The small cafe at the end of the road is hers.

Example:

The book is my. (incorrect)

The book is mine. (correct)

Hence, the correct option is (B).

5. The correct answer is- his tempers on.

There are some uncountable nouns that don't take the articles 'a/an', many, few, and plural form:

- Furniture, scenery, luggage, temper, hair, knowledge, equipment, pottery, music, jewellery, etc.

Correct sentence: He loses his temper on the slightest provocation.

Example:

The sceneries at my friend's house enchanted me. (incorrect)

The pieces of scenery at my friend's house enchanted me. (correct)

Hence, the correct option is (B).

6. The correct answer is- all the mouse.

Some nouns are not made plural by adding 's/es'. It is done in a different manner.

Criterion- criteria, mouse- mice, phenomenon- phenomena, radius- radii, syllabus- syllabi, etc.

Example: You don't fulfil the criteria set by the commission.

Correct Sentence: The man played the flute and led all the mice out of the town.

Hence, the correct option is (D).

7. The correct answer is- I didn't knew.

Let's look at some conjunctions that contain the inverted form of the verb apart from the interrogative sentences:

Example:

Hardly had I left the cinema hall than I saw the actor himself. (incorrect)

Hardly had I left the cinema hall when I saw the actor himself. (correct)

Whenever 'did' is used as an auxiliary verb, the main verb will be in 1st form.

Hence, the correct option is (D).

8. The correct answer is how can we.

Let's look at some conjunctions that contain the inverted form of the verb apart from the interrogative sentences:

'No sooner...than', 'Hardly/scarcely...when', etc.

For example:

Hardly had I left the cinema hall than I saw the actor himself. (incorrect)

Hardly had I left the cinema hall when I saw the actor himself. (correct)

Since the given sentence is assertive and doesn't contain any of the above-mentioned conjunctions, the use of the inverted form of the verb is wrong in the sentence.

Hence, the correct option is (C).

9. The correct answer is "by two days".

In the given sentence, the use of the preposition 'by' is incorrect. The preposition 'by' means not later than a particular time or date. The preposition 'within' should be used in place of 'by' as per the context of the sentence. The preposition 'within' means before the end of a period of time.

The correct sentence is: I want you to complete this work within two days.

Hence, the correct option is (A).

10. The correct answer is "as you".

In the given sentence, the use of the preposition 'as' is incorrect. The preposition 'as' means during the time of being (the thing specified).

The adverb 'when' should be used in place of 'as'. The adverb 'when' is used for talking about a particular time or situation.

The correct sentence is "You must be careful about what you say when you meet her."

Hence, the correct option is (A).

11. The correct answer is "a narrow street".

This sentence is talking about a street on which large trucks can enter despite it being narrow. Here, there is no comparison with other streets or there is no superlative being mentioned, the form 'a narrowest' is incorrect. Instead, 'a narrow' should be used to correctly convey the meaning.

The correct sentence is- Although this is a narrow street, many large trucks can enter it.

Hence, the correct option is (D).

12. The correct answer is- unless she.

In the given sentence, the use of the conjunction 'unless' is incorrect. The conjunction 'unless' means except if (used to introduce the case in which a statement being made is not true or valid).

The conjunction 'until' should be used in place of 'unless'. The conjunction 'until' means up to the point in time or the event mentioned.

So, the correct sentence is- Zoya won the first prize in the race until she stumbled and fell.

Hence, the correct option is (D).

13. The correct answer is for a hour.

In the given sentence, the noun 'hour' is unspecified. 'A' and 'an' are indefinite articles, which means that they refer to, or introduce, an unspecified noun. We use 'a' before a consonant sound, and we use 'an' before a vowel sound (here, hour).

So, the correct sentence is 'Do you mind lending me your book for an hour?'

Hence, the correct option is (B).

14. The correct answer is- is made from silver.

In the given sentence, the use of the preposition 'from' is incorrect. The preposition 'from' is used for indicating the raw material out of which something is manufactured.

The preposition 'of' should be used in place of 'from' as it is used for indicating the material or substance constituting something.

So, the correct sentence is 'This jewellery box is made of silver and is an antique piece.'

Hence, the correct option is (D).

15. The correct sentence is- 'There was enough evidence to convict him on the selling of fake medicines.'

In the given sentence, the use of the specified or particular noun 'selling' without any article is incorrect.

The definite article is used before singular and plural nouns when the noun is specific or particular. Therefore, the definite article 'the' should be used before the specific noun 'selling'.

Hence, the correct option is (A).

16. The correct answer is- 'waiting at the airport'.

We know that in the given sentence 'travellers' are nouns. And 'tired' and 'vexed' are the adjectives.

Here, 'waiting' is used as a main verb. But the helping verb is missing. The given sentence is in the past tense. Therefore, 'were' will be used here as the helping verb.

So, the correct sentence is- 'The tired and vexed travellers were waiting at the airport for a long time.'

Hence, the correct option is (A).

17. The correct sentence is- 'The venue for the wedding has not been finalized yet.'

In a sentence helping verb should be used according to the main subject of the sentence. In the given sentence the main subject is 'The venue' and it is singular. Therefore, a singular helping verb should be used.

Hence, the correct option is (C).

18. The correct answer is- 'since it's formation'.

The erroneous part 'since it's formation' will be 'since its formation'. It's is a contraction of "it is" or "it has."

Whereas, 'Its' is a possessive determiner we use to say that something belongs to or refers to something. Here, in the given question possessive case that is 'its' should be used because it is talking about the formation of the club.

So, the correct sentence is- 'She has been a member of this club since its formation.'

Hence, the correct option is (B).

19. The correct answer is- 'come to the'.

If we carefully examine the sentence, we can easily figure out that it is talking about an incident of the past. Thus, we will use the simple past tense 'came' instead of 'come'.

So, the correct sentence is- 'No one of them came to the inauguration of our new factory.'

Hence, the correct option is (A).

20. The correct answer is- 'shouted out to each another'.

The erroneous Part 'shouted out to each another' will be 'shouted out to 'one another'.

The given sentence is an example of Reciprocal Pronoun. We know that 'each other' is used when there are two people.

- Example: Bill and Ted are being excellent to each other.

This means Bill is being excellent to Ted, and Ted is being excellent to Bill. They're practicing what you might call excellence reciprocity.

We know that when we are talking about more than two people, we should use a different reciprocal pronoun that is 'one another'.

- Example: People need to know one another to be at their honest best.

In the given sentence 'The three' is the subject and with them, we should use 'one another'. So, the correct sentence is: The three of them shouted out to one another when the train started moving.

Hence, the correct option is (C).

21. The correct sentence is "A closed economy is identified as a human community that produces all it consumes and **consumes** all it produces".

The error is in the last part of the sentence 'and consumed all it produces'. The sentence is in the present tense and hence the second form of the verb (consumed) is incorrect. The verb should be used in the present tense (consume) in accordance with the entire statement.

Hence, the correct option is (D).

22. The correct sentence is "Iron is the most useful **of** all metals".

The error is in the last part of the sentence 'against all metals'.

The preposition 'of' is used when referring to or relating to something. Iron is metal itself and contextually the sentence means that iron is the most useful among all the metals. To make the sentence correct against must be replaced with 'of'.

Hence, the correct option is (C).

23. The correct sentence is "While every care **has** been taken in preparing the results, the company reserves the right to correct any inadvertent errors at a later stage".

The error lies in the first part of the sentence 'while every care have been taken.'

In the given sentence the subject 'care' is an abstract noun, so it will be followed by a singular verb (has). The plural verb (have) is incorrectly used in the given sentence. It must be replaced with 'has' to make the sentence correct.

Hence, the correct option is (A).

24. The correct sentence is "My sister and **I** are planning a trip from Jaipur to Delhi".

The error is in the first part of the sentence 'My sister and me are.'

'Me' is an objective case of the pronoun 'I'. So that we can say that it is incorrect here because we need a subjective case. So it must be replaced with the subjective case 'I' to make the sentence correct.

Hence, the correct option is (A).

25. The correct sentence is "Despite the thrill of winning the lottery last week, my neighbour still seems **happy**".

The error is in the fourth part of the sentence 'still seems happily'. The usage of 'happily' is incorrect in the given sentence. To make the sentence correct replace the adverb 'happily' with the adjective 'happy'.

According to the rule of grammar, seems is a linking verb and with a linking verb, we need to write an adjective (happy) and not an adverb (happily). For example: The eggs smell **rotten**. Here 'rotten' is an adjective.

Hence, the correct option is (D).

26. The correct sentence is "Children are not allowed to use the swimming pool unless they are with an adult.

The sentence is error-free and grammatically correct. As both the plural subjects (children and they) are followed by the plural verb (are). The conjunction 'unless' is also correctly used in the sentence.

Hence, the correct option is (D).

27. The correct sentence is "Her knowledge of Indian languages **is** far beyond the common".

The error lies in the last part of the sentence 'are far beyond the common.'

Knowledge is an uncountable noun and hence the usage of the plural verb 'are' is incorrect. It must be replaced with the singular verb 'is' to make the sentence correct.

Hence, the correct option is (C).

28. The correct sentence is "You look as if you have **run** all the way home".

The error is in the second part of the sentence 'you have ran.'

The given sentence is in the present perfect tense and expresses a finished action with a result in the present. In perfect tense, we shall use the 3rd form of the verb run. The three forms of the verb 'run' are: run - ran - run. Thus the usage of the verb 'ran' is incorrect and must be replaced with 'run'.

Hence, the correct option is (B).

29. The correct sentence is "The real voyage of discovery consists not in seeking new landscapes, but in having new eyes".

The error lies in the second part of the sentence 'consist not in seeking new landscapes.'

As per the subject-verb agreement, the verb agrees with the subject in number and person. The subject (voyage) is singular and hence the corresponding verb (consist) must also be singular. So 'consist' should be replaced with 'consists' to agree with the singular subject.

Hence, the correct option is (B).

30. The correct sentence is "No struggle can ever **succeed** without women participating side by side with men".

The error lies in the first part of the sentence 'No struggle can ever succeeded.'

The verb 'succeeded' is incorrectly used. It should be replaced with the first form of the verb 'succeed'. As we know that after the modal verb we always use the first form of the main verb.

Hence, the correct option is (A).

Ques (1-2):Direction: In the sentence, a word is underlined followed by four words/groups of words. Select the option that is nearest in meaning to the underlined word and choose the correct option.

Q.1 This is akin to a contractual relationship that places obligations on the entities entrusted with data.

A. Removed **B.** Narrow
C. Similar **D.** Unparallel

Q.2 The manner in which this exercise has been undertaken leaves much to be desired.

A. Dislike **B.** Unlikely
C. Wish for **D.** Asked for

Q.3 Direction: In the sentence, a word is underlined followed by four words/groups of words. Select the option that is opposite in meaning to the underlined word and choose the correct option.

Beauty lies in the eyes of the beholder.

A. Allure **B.** Charm
C. Inelegance **D.** Ideal

Q.4 Direction: In the given sentence, a word is underlined followed by four words/groups of words. Select the option that is opposite In meaning to the underlined word and choose the correct option.

He has been facing a kind of intimidation by his friends for last two years.

A. Wiles **B.** Conviction
C. Persuasion **D.** Support

Q.5 Direction: The following sentence consists an underlined word followed by four options. Select the option that is opposite in meaning to the underlined word and mark your response accordingly.

The decision was absurd for many of the members of the team.

[Indian Military Academy (IMA), 2021], [Officers Training Academy (OTA), 2021]

A. bizarre **B.** meaningless
C. reasonable **D.** thoughtful

Q.6 Direction: The following sentence consists an underlined word followed by four options. Select the option that is opposite in meaning to the underlined word and mark your response accordingly.

Twenty first century has turned out to be a century of problems contrary to the thinking that it would be a better time.

A. Similar **B.** Different
C. Divergent **D.** Faith

Q.7 Direction: The following sentence consists an underlined word followed by four options. Select the option that is opposite in meaning to the underlined word and mark your response accordingly.

Language is an instrument for asserting one's identity, attitude and perspective.

A. Declaring **B.** Supporting
C. Denying **D.** Propagating

Ques (8-14):

Direction: Question consists of a sentence with an underlined word followed by four words. Select the option that is nearest in meaning to the underlined word and mark your answer.

Q.8 Her dynamic nature impressed everyone.

[UPSC NDA, 2021]

A. Enduring **B.** Attentive
C. Evolutionary **D.** Jealous

Q.9 She was lamenting her destiny.

[UPSC NDA, 2021]

A. Celebrating **B.** Bemoaning
C. Blaming **D.** Making

Q.10 Under his leadership the company grew in an organic manner.

[UPSC NDA, 2021]

A. Natural **B.** Speedy
C. Unusual **D.** Disciplined

Q.11 He is always anxious.

[UPSC NDA, 2019]

A. Worried **B.** Dispassionate
C. Sluggish **D.** Torpid

Q.12 A human being is always vulnerable to other human beings:

A. Resilient **B.** Elastic
C. Defenseless **D.** Crude

Q.13 The Managing Director of the company declared that he is broke and there is a need to seek support from the government:

A. Bankrupt **B.** Rich
C. Making profit **D.** Having liabilities

Q.14 He loves doing nasty things.

A. Nice **B.** Fastidious
C. Foul **D.** Finicky

Ques (15-18):Direction: Select the most appropriate synonym of the given word.

Q.15 ACCURATELY

A. Moderately **B.** Correctly
C. Promptly **D.** Partially

Q.16 CONDESCENDING

A. Stimulating **B.** Accusing
C. Creating **D.** Patronizing

Q.17 PLEASANT

A. Tiresome **B.** Tedious
C. Refreshing **D.** Exasperating

Q.18 TENACITY

A. Idleness **B.** Timidity
C. Firmness **D.** Cowardice

Q.19 Direction: Select the most appropriate antonym of the given word.

DEJECTED

A. Moody **B.** Doleful **C.** Morose **D.** Cheerful

Q.20 Direction: Select the most appropriate antonym of the given word.

MEDDLE

A. Prize **B.** Fortify **C.** Support **D.** Ignore

Ques (21-23):Direction: In the given sentence a word is given in bold and is followed by four words. Select the word that is most similar in meaning to the underlined word.

Q.21 Even though the invite mentioned 'Black Tie optional', everyone at the party looked very <u>elegant</u>.

A. Disappointed **B.** Graceful
C. Disgusting **D.** Repugnant

Q.22 The students were asked to provide a <u>synopsis</u> of the story by the weekend.

A. Conclusion **B.** Paragraph
C. Redaction **D.** Summary

Q.23 The machinery that David had installed 5 years ago had become quite <u>obsolete.</u>

A. Current **B.** Efficient
C. Neglected **D.** Outdated

Q.24 Direction: Select the most appropriate synonym of the given word.

FOSTERING

A. Safeguarding **B.** Neglecting
C. Ignoring **D.** Nurturing

Ques (25-30):Direction: Select the most appropriate antonym of the given word.

Q.25 Foremost

A. Hindmost **B.** Disposed
C. Mature **D.** Premature

Q.26 Protect

A. Defend **B.** Deprive **C.** Desert **D.** Devise

Q.27 Beautiful

A. Wonderful **B.** Graceful
C. Ugly **D.** Handsome

Q.28 Mighty

A. Forcible **B.** Weak **C.** Forceful **D.** Tough

Q.29 Glory

A. Splendour **B.** Notoriety
C. Fame **D.** Debasement

Q.30 Underhand

A. Hidden **B.** Surreptitious
C. Obscure **D.** Exposed

// Smart Answer Sheet //

Correct Indicates percentage of students who answered questions correctly.

Skipped Indicates percentage of students who skipped questions.

Q.	Ans.	Correct	Skipped
1	C	84.9 %	14.04 %
2	C	87.79 %	11.04 %
3	C	82.39 %	15.66 %
4	C	77.63 %	16.3 %
5	C	79.54 %	20.08 %
6	A	77.88 %	15.38 %
7	C	77.82 %	17.99 %
8	C	80.57 %	13.24 %
9	B	86.83 %	12.53 %
10	A	76.53 %	23.13 %
11	A	79.08 %	15.82 %
12	C	85.11 %	10.15 %
13	A	86.79 %	10.83 %
14	C	76.51 %	18.39 %
15	B	76.09 %	12.44 %
16	D	79.6 %	16.28 %
17	C	78.62 %	13.01 %
18	C	76.44 %	15.57 %
19	D	85.47 %	12.98 %
20	D	88.41 %	11.42 %
21	B	89.95 %	10.0 %
22	D	87.44 %	12.21 %
23	D	89.26 %	10.36 %
24	D	80.08 %	14.91 %
25	B	81.49 %	15.32 %
26	C	86.6 %	11.49 %
27	C	80.94 %	15.91 %
28	B	83.36 %	14.26 %
29	D	84.94 %	13.71 %
30	D	89.41 %	10.48 %

Performance Analysis	
Avg. Score (%)	60.0%
Toppers Score (%)	70.0%
Your Score	

//Hints and Solutions//

1. The correct synonym of akin is similar.

Akin: of similar character; related by blood; related, close.

For example: This game is closely akin to rugby.

Similar: having a resemblance in appearance, character or quantity; without being identical.

For example: I would have reacted in a similar way if it had happened to me.

Hence, the correct option is (C).

2. The correct synonym of desired is wish for.

Desired: strongly wished for or intended, to find somebody or something really attractive.

For example: Their strategy produced the desired outcome.

Wish for: feel or express a strong desire or hope for something, desire, want

For example: We know what she'll be wishing for on her birthday.

Hence, the correct option is (C).

3. The correct opposite word of beauty is inelegance.

Beauty: a combination of qualities, such as shape, colour, or form, that pleases the aesthetic senses, especially the sight.

For example: We explored the natural beauty of the island.

Inelegance: the quality or state of being inelegant; lack of elegance, ungrateful.

For example: Dean caught his breath before answering her inelegant question.

Hence, the correct option is (C).

4. The correct opposite word of intimidation is persuasion.

Intimidation: the action of intimidating someone, or the state of being intimidated, frightened, or scared.

For example: She then rashly tried intimidation and threatened to espouse the cause of Britannicus.

Persuasion: the action or process of persuading someone or of being persuaded to do or believe something.

For example: I had to use a little gentle persuasion to get her to agree.

Hence, the correct option is (C).

5. The correct opposite word of absurd is reasonable.

Absurd: wildly unreasonable, illogical, or inappropriate.

Reasonable: (of a person) having sound judgment; fair and sensible.

Let's look at the meanings of the other given options:

bizarre- very strange or unusual, especially so as to cause interest or amusement

meaningless- having no meaning or significance

thoughtful- absorbed in or involving thought

Thus, from the given meanings, we find that absurd and reasonable are antonyms.

Hence, the correct option is (C).

6. The correct opposite word of contrary is similar.

Contrary: opposite in nature, direction, or meaning

Similar: resembling without being identical

Let's look at the meanings of the other given options:

Different- not the same as another or each other; unlike in nature, form, or quality

Divergent- tending to be different or develop in different directions

Faith- complete trust or confidence in someone or something

Thus, from the given meanings, we find that contrary and similar are antonyms.

Hence, the correct option is (A).

7. The correct opposite of asserting is denying.

Asserting: state a fact or belief confidently and forcefully

Denying: state that one refuses to admit the truth or existence of

Let's look at the meanings of the other given options:

Declaring- say something in a solemn and emphatic manner

Supporting- bear all or part of the weight of; hold up

Propagating- breed specimens of (a plant or animal) by natural processes from the parent stock.

Hence, the correct option is (C).

8. The word 'evolutionary' is nearest in meaning to the underlined word 'dynamic'.

The meaning of the given words:

Dynamic: continuously changing or developing.

Evolutionary: involving a gradual process of change and development.

Enduring: lasting over a period of time, durable.

Attentive: paying close attention to something.

Jealous: feeling or showing an envious resentment of someone or their achievements, possessions, or perceived advantages.

Hence, the correct option is (C).

9. The word 'bemoaning' is nearest in meaning to the underlined word 'lamenting'.

The meaning of the given words:

Lamenting: expressing regret or disappointment about something.

Bemoaning: expressing discontent or sorrow over (something).

Celebrating: acknowledging (a significant or happy day or event) with a social gathering or enjoyable activity.

Blaming: feeling or declaring that (someone or something) is responsible for a fault or wrong.

Making: forming (something) by putting parts together or combining substances, create.

Hence, the correct option is (B).

10. The word 'natural' is nearest in meaning to the underlined word 'organic'.

The meaning of the given words:

Organic: not using artificial chemicals in the production of plants and animals for food, natural.

Natural: as found in nature and not involving anything made or done by people, organic.

Speedy: done or occurring quickly.

Unusual: not habitually or commonly occurring or done.

Disciplined: showing a controlled form of behaviour or way of working.

Hence, the correct option is (A).

11. The option that is nearest in meaning to the underlined word 'anxious' is 'worried'.

Anxious means feeling or showing worry, nervousness, or unease about something.

Worried means anxious or troubled about actual or potential problems.

Hence, the correct option is (A).

12. The option that is nearest in meaning to the underlined word 'vulnerable' is 'defenseless'.

Vulnerable means exposed to the possibility of being attacked or harmed, either physically or emotionally.

Defenseless means without defense or protection; totally vulnerable.

Hence, the correct option is (C).

13. The option that is nearest in meaning to the underlined word 'broke' is 'bankrupt'.

Bankrupt means declared in law as unable to pay their debts.

Broke means having completely run out of money.

Hence, the correct option is (A).

14. The option that is nearest in meaning to the underlined word 'nasty' is 'foul'.

Nasty means very bad or unpleasant.

Foul means having a disgusting smell or taste or being dirty.

Hence, the correct option is (C).

15. Accurately and correctly are synonymous to each other.

Accurately: in a way that is correct, exact, and without any mistakes

Correctly: in a way that is in agreement with the true facts or with what is generally accepted

Moderately: in a way that is neither small nor large in size, amount, degree, or strength

Promptly: done quickly and without delay

Partially: not completely

Hence, the correct option is (B).

16. Condescending and patronizing are synonymous to each other.

Condescending: showing or characterized by a patronizing or superior attitude toward others

Patronizing: speaking or behaving towards someone as if they are stupid or not important

Stimulating: encouraging or arousing interest or enthusiasm

Accusing: indicating a belief in someone's guilt or culpability

Creating: bringing something into existence

Hence, the correct option is (D).

17. The most appropriate synonym of the given word 'Pleasant' is 'Refreshing'.

Pleasant: enjoyable, attractive, friendly, or easy to like

Refreshing: making you feel less hot or tired

Tiresome: annoying and making you lose patience

Tedious: boring and tiring, esp. because long or often repeated

Exasperating: annoying, because we can do nothing to solve a problem

Hence, the correct option is (C).

18. The synonyms of the word 'Tenacity' are "firmness, bravery, courage".

The word 'Tenacity' means the quality or fact of being very determined; determination.

The word 'firmness' means resolute determination and strength of character.

Hence, the correct option is (C).

19. The antonyms of the word 'Dejected' are "cheerful, delighted, happy".

The word 'Dejected' means feeling unhappiness.

The word 'cheerful' means noticeably happy and optimistic.

Hence, the correct option is (D).

20. The correct antonym of meddle is ignore.

Meddle- to interest oneself in what is not one's concern

Ignore- refuse to take notice of or acknowledge, disregard intentionally

Prize- a thing given as a reward to the winner of a competition or in recognition of an outstanding achievement

Fortify- provide (a place) with defensive works as a protection against attack

Support- bear all or part of the weight of, hold up

Hence, the correct option is (D).

21. It is clear that elegant and graceful are similar terms.

Elegant: Stylish and tasteful in appearance

Graceful: Being stylish and refined in appearance

E.g. Despite having injured herself badly during practice, Serena played in a graceful manner.

Hence, the correct option is (B).

22. It is clear that 'synopsis' and 'summary' are similar words.

Synopsis: A brief or general summary of something

Summary: A brief statement or account of something, the main points

Hence, the correct option is (D).

23. It is clear that 'obsolete' and 'outdated' are similar words.

Obsolete: no longer produced or used; out of date.

Outdated: out of date

Hence, the correct option is (D).

24. Synonym of Fostering is Nurturing.

Nurturing : care for and protect (someone or something) while they are growing.

Fostering : encourage the development of (something, especially something desirable).

Safeguarding : a measure taken to protect someone or something or to prevent something undesirable.

Neglecting : fail to care for properly.

Ignoring : refuse to take notice of or acknowledge; disregard intentionally.

Hence, the correct option is (D).

25. Foremost and disposed are antonyms of each other.

Foremost : most prominent in rank, importance, or position.

Disposed : inclined or willing.

Hindmost : furthest back, latest or ultramodern.

Mature : fully developed physically, full-grown.

Premature : occurring or done before the usual or proper time, too early.

Hence, the correct option is (B).

26. Protect and desert are antonyms of each other.

Protect: keep safe from harm.

Desert: to abandon that is to stop supporting or looking after.

Defend: protect from harm or danger.

Deprive: prevent (a person or place) from having or using something

Devise: plan or invent (a complex procedure, system, or mechanism) by careful thought

Hence, the correct option is (C).

27. Ugly posses opposite meaning of Beautiful.

Wonderful, Graceful, Handsome and Marvelous are more or less synonyms of Beautiful.

Hence, the correct option is (C).

28. The antonym of mighty is weak.

Weak: having little strength or energy; not strong.

Mighty : possessing great and impressive power or strength.

Forcible : done by force.

Forceful : strong and assertive, vigorous and powerful.

Tough : strong enough to withstand adverse conditions or rough handling.

Hence, the correct option is (B).

29. The antonym of glory is debasment.

Debasement : reduce (something) in quality or value, degrade.

Glory : high renown or honour won by notable achievements, upgrade.

Splendour : magnificent and splendid appearance, grandeur.

Notoriety : the state of being famous or well known for some bad quality or deed.

Fame : the state of being known by many people.

Hence, the correct option is (D).

30. The antonym of underhand is exposed.

Underhand: marked by secrecy, chicanery, and deception, not honest and aboveboard.

Exposed : make (something) visible by uncovering it.

Hidden : kept out of sight, concealed.

Surreptitious : kept secret, especially because it would not be approved of.

Obscure : not discovered or known about, uncertain.

Hidden, Surreptitious, Obscure and Underhand are more or less synonyms to each other.

Hence, the correct option is (D).

// Notes //

// Notes //

www.ingramcontent.com/pod-product-compliance
Ingram Content Group UK Ltd.
Pitfield, Milton Keynes, MK11 3LW, UK
UKHW061705190726
13853UKWH00008B/2407

9 789355 560780